"Can You Or Can You Not Teach Someone To Read In Three Weeks?" Sam asked.

Leslie was furious. "How do you expect me to answer that without knowing the child? It depends on what kind of person he is, how willing he is, whether I can build up a rapport—"

"The 'child' is willing to put in twenty-hour days for the next three weeks."

Leslie jumped to her feet. "I should have expected this. Children are not machines, Buster. If you brought me here expecting to treat a child like a computer—"

"This child is a machine. He's also a living, breathing embarrassment to the government of this country."

"Anyone who thinks of a child as an embarrassment is a pompous creep as far as I'm concerned. I've never heard such an inhuman, cruel, insensitive—"

"The child, lady, is me." He glared at her, "I'm the one with the reading problem."

Dear Reader,

Welcome to Silhouette! Our goal is to give you hours of unbeatable reading pleasure, and we hope you'll enjoy each month's six new Silhouette Desires. These sensual, provocative love stories are both believable and compelling—sometimes they're poignant, sometimes humorous, but always enjoyable.

Indulge yourself. Experience all the passion and excitement of falling in love along with our heroine as she meets the irresistible man of her dreams and together they overcome all obstacles in the path to a happy ending.

If this is your first Desire, I hope it'll be the first of many. If you're already a Silhouette Desire reader, thanks for your support! Look for some of your favorite authors in the coming months: Stephanie James, Diana Palmer, Dixie Browning, Ann Major and Doreen Owens Malek, to name just a few.

Happy reading!

Isabel Swift
Senior Editor

SDRL-7/85

JENNIFER GREENE
Dear Reader

Silhouette Desire

Published by Silhouette Books New York

America's Publisher of Contemporary Romance

SILHOUETTE BOOKS
300 East 42nd St., New York, N.Y. 10017

ISBN: 0-373-05350-9

First Silhouette Books printing May 1987

America's Publisher of Contemporary Romance

Printed in the U.S.A.

Books by Jennifer Greene

Silhouette Desire

Body and Soul #263
Foolish Pleasure #293
Madam's Room #326
Dear Reader #350

JENNIFER GREENE

lives near Lake Michigan. Born in Grosse Pointe, she moved to a farm when she married her husband fifteen years ago. Jennifer feels that love needs both laughter and tribulations to grow. She's won the *Romantic Times* award for Sensuality and the RWA Silver Medallion, and also writes under the name of Jeanne Grant.

One

"Of course I believe you," Leslie said smoothly. "And I would absolutely love to do this little secret mission for the government, Mr....?"

"Harry. Just make it Harry. I—"

"Harry," Leslie said lovingly. "Wonderful name. Listen, Harry. I'm going to go in the house and get you a nice tall glass of lemonade, okay? You just sit right here and relax. Don't worry about a thing. Think about James Bond movies," she encouraged as she edged carefully toward her back door. Inside—just inside, thank God—was a telephone.

She wasn't exactly frightened. Granted that the little man had half scared her out of her wits when he'd popped up in her yard twenty minutes ago, twisting his hat in his hands and talking about patriotism. Now that it was June, the old Victorian house she'd converted to a school was completely deserted. There wasn't a neighbor within a half mile and that made screaming for help rather useless—if Leslie were the screaming type, which she wasn't.

She was unhappy when her strange gentleman swiftly moved to block her entrance to the back door. "Miss Stuart, as I said, I've been trying to reach you by telephone for days. I never meant to scare you by coming directly in your yard, but when you never answered your phone—"

"You didn't scare me," she assured him. "Please don't get upset."

"I'm not upset. And I know you don't believe me, but I'm telling you I'm serious. You're in the unique position of being qualified to perform a very special service for your government."

"Of course I am," Leslie said soothingly. Just like horses could fly. She strove for patience . . . and to comprehend exactly what kind of maniac she had on her hands.

Delusions seemed to be his chief problem—although that tendency was not one that struck her as unusual in the male species. In this case, though, the man did an exceptional job of looking harmless. His paunchy cheeks sagged in the heat, and his wrinkled gray suit looked as if he'd lived in it for days. His short stocky frame was topped by wispy gray hair, baby-blue eyes and a thin little mouth. Frankly, he looked too darned tired to be your average pervert. His behavior was even rather...endearing. He'd asked twice if she were really the schoolteacher named Leslie Stuart, turned beet red when his eyes had focused on her halter top, and hadn't stopped mopping his forehead with the edge of a grimy handkerchief since.

To her advantage, Leslie had known for years that "harmless" and "man" never came in the same package, and a man Harry's size was not likely to threaten a woman who, like herself, was skilled in self-defense. The issue was simply how to get rid of the nut before it came to using her skills.

"Look, if we could just go inside and sit down, Miss Stuart. I could explain about this job—"

"Oh, I don't think we need to go inside," she demurred quickly. "It's a wonderful day out here, don't you think? So nice and warm." He'd flashed fairly authentic-looking ID in her face, which was disturbing. She couldn't imagine how he'd gotten ahold of a card with State Department etched on it.

"If you would just listen to me—"

"There now, I'm listening." She smiled encouragingly and perched at the top of her porch steps. "Really, I was listening before. I'm delighted to hear that the government's so desperate for schoolteachers."

"We're *not* desperate for schoolteachers," he rasped in frustration.

"Now, don't get upset again—"

"I am *not* upset." It was so hot he couldn't breathe. And he'd been expecting a schoolmarm type, not a nearly naked amazon mowing her lawn barefoot. Her pink shorts weren't decent and every damn time she moved he was terrified she was going to lose the top she was wearing altogether. Her froth of silvery-blond hair made him think of a fallen angel; her sultry laugh could make a monk perspire; and she had huge, sulky dark eyes. When Harry got back to Wyoming, he was going to kill Pierce. And retire once and for all. Enough was enough. "Look," he said wearily. "Like I said, I'm prepared to pay you all expenses and three thousand dollars just for three weeks of your time."

"Sure you are." She patted his knee.

"*And* we'll chip in new equipment for your school. You've had a small problem getting financing recently—"

Leslie's eyes narrowed, just slightly. The little sweetheart was starting to grate on her nerves. It was no secret that she ran a local school, but she didn't like strangers prying into her affairs. Particularly male strangers.

"All you have to do is come with me for three weeks. The nature of the work we need you to do is nothing difficult, nothing dangerous, nothing you aren't uniquely qualified to do. I wish I could give you more information than that—I *can* give you several telephone numbers to call that will verify everything I've told you—but secrecy is absolutely essential."

"I love a good mystery," Leslie said affectionately. "Read a lot of suspense recently, Harry? Ah!" She clicked her fingers. "Shouldn't you have checked out my security clearance?"

He stared at her.

She smiled. "I watch a lot of spy flicks, too," she confessed conspiratorially. "Love 'em. And this is really lots of fun. To tell you the truth, I'm honored you went to all this trouble just for me. If I didn't have the rest of the yard to mow, I'd be glad to listen to you all afternoon, Harry, but really..." She stood up.

"Your specialty is oculomotor dysfunction in pursuits," he said desperately.

Leslie hesitated. Not too many people blithely threw around such terms unless they were familiar with them.

"You've had outstanding results with eccentric fixations and strabismic amblyopia...."

Her throat was suddenly oddly dry. This was all becoming just a little too real. "Harry—"

"Five thousand dollars," he pressed frantically. "Five thousand dollars for three lousy weeks of your time. And if you get me a list I'll have that equipment *inside* your school in three days. Will that convince you to at least sit down and talk to me, Miss Stuart? What the hell have you got to lose?"

* * *

Leslie looked out the plane window and saw the Tetons' jagged peaks looming closer. From a distance the mountains had looked majestic, awesome, still. The nearer they came, the more she was conscious of wilderness. These were no docile, rolling hills but country a man could never tame. The Cessna's twin engines droned in her ears. She lifted the cup of tea she had in her hand and took a soothing sip, glancing at Harry.

He was seated at the opposite window. Even though it was only early afternoon, the glass in his hand held straight whiskey. Though his shirt was clean, he was still wearing the same wrinkled gray business suit she'd seen him in three days ago. He didn't appear to have any other clothes, and his forehead still broke out in perspiration whenever she smiled at him.

Leslie had smiled at him a lot over the past three days. Call it the devil in her character.

She finished the tea, set the cup down and closed her eyes. In her mind's eye, she could still see the seven thousand dollars' worth of crated diagnostic equipment now sitting in her front hall. Harry was under the silly impression that she'd agreed to go with him because of those crates. He was wrong. Though she badly wanted the equipment for her school, the issue was much simpler. Leslie had never turned down a child who needed her help.

All she'd been able to get out of Harry was that they were going to a cabin near Jackson Hole in the Tetons for three weeks and that it had something to do with the government and a man named Pierce. Harry repeatedly looked confused whenever she asked him about a child—but then Harry was very good at his job.

Leslie wasn't a fool. Her only claim to modest fame was an unprecedented success rate with learning-disabled children—there was no other reason anyone would have sought her out. The rest of the business was both confusing and infuriating. She had no idea why the government was involved, why on earth they didn't just bring the child to her school, or why they were willing to go to this incredible expense.

Leslie absently thought that when one got the government involved in anything, confusion wasn't so surprising. She had nothing specifically against the government—except that it was run by far too many men. In her experience, men loved to keep their little secrets, act self-important and flaunt their egos whenever possible.

Leslie had learned all about men's egos when she was sixteen. Some lessons in life one never forgot, and at twenty-nine she was really very good with men. Harry, for instance, had no idea she was annoyed by all this secrecy or suffering from a sick feeling of nerves. He was too busy being terrified of her.

Across the aisle, he said carefully, "We'll be landing in a few minutes. You'd better..." He motioned to her seat belt, accidentally let his eyes land on her breasts and turned a sweet shade of dull pink.

Leslie flicked the two metal bits of the seat belt together and grinned. Poor Harry. He was still waiting for her to dress like a schoolteacher. But whether he knew it or not, she was wearing a kind of uniform. Her white jeans molded beautifully over sleek long legs and her sandals showed off bare toes with nails painted a sexy red. Her scarlet cotton top had crisscrosses for a back, which made it impossible for her to wear a bra. She wouldn't have worn one anyway.

Leslie felt rather ruthless about her figure. A woman needed every weapon she had in life to survive. Men were ceaselessly diverted by breasts—rather silly, really, all women had them—and when a man was looking below her neck, she always had ample opportunity to look above his. It hadn't taken her long to figure out Harry.

After shamelessly flirting with him for the past three days, she had the poor man regularly popping antacid tablets. He was so careful not to touch her that one would think her skin was wired for bombs. Not a man anywhere could ever guess she'd been celibate for years. Certainly not the three men she was currently juggling in her private life. Harry was a cupcake by comparison.

She would undoubtedly have behaved better if she hadn't been so irritated. If she were going to deal with a child with a unique set of problems, she needed to know about him or her. She was specifically dying of curiosity as to what made the child—or his parents—so special that they rated all this underhanded cloak-and-dagger nonsense.

The plane rolled to a stop. A glance out the window yielded a view of a grassy landing strip in a valley between mountains—and not a building in sight. "There'll be a Jeep waiting for us," Harry told Leslie nervously. He said a private word to the pilot and then slid the plane doors open.

Less than ten minutes later the plane was airborne again, without them. Leslie's two pieces of luggage were in the back of a battered old Jeep. Harry was in the driver's seat beside her, looking sick and hassled and holding a handkerchief in front of her face. "I'm afraid you have to wear this over your eyes."

"You're not serious," she informed him.

"I'm afraid I am. Please," he said apologetically. "It isn't that far a drive, and it's terribly important you not be able to tell anyone where we are."

"Of all the ridiculous, childish..." Men! She grabbed the handkerchief. When she whipped it around her eyes, she could hear the crinkle of tinfoil, and knew Harry was popping another antacid.

"I know, I know. But it's for your country, Miss Stuart."

"*Leslie,*" she corrected him furiously.

"Yes. Leslie. Try and remember this is all for a good cause, and we're really very grateful."

The Jeep jolted and jogged on the rugged mountain road like a bumper car at a carnival. All Leslie could think of was that the male breed was incapable of simple honesty. She smelled the fresh green pines, felt a hot sun flickering on her head, inhaled the heady mountain air... and tried to calm down. Under any other circumstances, she would have loved a three-week vacation in the mountains.

During the school year she worked sixteen-hour days. The children were everything to her. The nasty, rebellious ones were her favorites—the ones whom the regular school system had labeled stupid, the ones who flaunted authority and sulked in their seats and stared at her, daring her to turn them into readers. Leslie loved that dare. She loved the kids, but by the time June finally wandered onto the calendar, she was normally ready for two months of rest and peace. Summers were usually spent hiking alone in the wild regions of northern Minnesota, sunbathing nude and alone behind her tall fence and puttering with the flowers in her garden. Those flowers were going to be totally neglected in her absence.

She frowned beneath the blindfold just as the Jeep braked to a stop. Not moving a muscle, she simply sat there.

"I...um...you can take it off now," Harry said meekly.

Her tone was cheerful. "You're sure?"

"Yes."

She slipped off the handkerchief, handed it to him and put out her hands. "You're going to handcuff me before we go in?"

Harry flushed. "No, of course not. You're perfectly free from here on."

"No need to frisk me for hidden weapons?" she insisted, and shook her head in mock despair. "Really, Harry, I think you're being more than a little lax. You didn't even go through my suitcases. For all you know I could have hidden a bazooka in my underpants. Assuming, of course," she said thoughtfully, "that I wear underpants."

His dull-pink cheeks acquired two dots of brick red. He closed his eyes and groped for the front pocket of his shirt. "Pierce has got to be in the house somewhere," he muttered.

Leslie climbed out of the Jeep, somewhat ashamed of herself for teasing him. The little man was just trying to do his job—whatever it was—and she'd certainly done nothing to help him. The truth was, she was always inclined to flash a little extra bravado when she was scared silly.

All her life she'd brazenly faced the worst of life's challenges with that particular trick—to flaunt what she was afraid of, never back down and never show weakness. Harry didn't scare her, an unknown child didn't scare her, and she couldn't think of a situation on earth where she couldn't take care of herself. But goose bumps had been climbing all over her flesh ever since the plane landed.

She pushed her hands in her pockets and looked around. The "cabin" was actually a handsome two-story wood and glass structure perched on the crest of a ravine. Somewhere she could hear flowing water. She saw no road, no other buildings. The mountains isolated the hideaway in privacy, and the house was surrounded by Douglas firs, spruces and rambling evergreen oaks. The picture was luxuriously peaceful. The place smelled like rich dark earth, like green, like sweet silence. She loved it just that fast . . . but the goose bumps kept coming.

She could always leave, she reminded herself. She was no stranger to wild country; and she'd packed a compass and some hastily assembled survival equipment. She was here only because she'd never turned away a kid in her life and didn't intend to start now. But if there was something out of kilter about this whole business, she wouldn't hesitate to take a private hike down the Tetons if she had to. There's nothing to be nervous about, she chastised herself.

At the sound of voices, she turned her head. The door stood ajar where Harry had disappeared in the house. Just inside, she could make out the tall shadow of a man. Pierce, she thought. The one major unknown in the whole business.

But of course, she did know him. Harry's secretiveness about the other man had told her everything she needed to know. Pierce was the mastermind behind this idiotic plan, the egomaniac who thought privacy was so critical, the self-important boob who believed he had to bribe a schoolteacher to come here when Leslie would cheerfully have come free and paid her own fare if they'd been honest with her about the child. Harry had been treated like an angel compared with how she intended to treat Pierce.

Harry's voice ceased, and she moved toward the door. Before she reached the first step, the tall shadow took substance.

She had to admit that that first impression took her aback. Expecting an overconfident peacock of a man, she got a long lion with tawny-gold hair. His angular features were sculpted with a strong brush— a slash of cheekbones, a blade of a jaw, a thick arch of sandy brows. His build was lean and his mouth compressed in a hard line. She thought of the power contained in steel. She thought of a man who went after what he wanted without ever looking back. She thought of a man's passion for control.

Her spine instantly stiffened. Leslie's instinct for judging men was finely tuned, honed like the blade of a knife. Certain men could be handled; certain men couldn't. In two seconds flat, she knew she didn't like Pierce.

The feeling appeared mutual. He had incredible gray eyes that burned with life, intelligence, restlessness and an intensity that disturbed her. Those eyes—clay and steel were of like color, yet one was pliable and the other never. His assessing gaze burned on hers for all of a minute. She sensed a massive irritation that surpassed even her own, and then he was moving forward with the quiet step of a man one never heard coming. "Miss Stuart? I'm Sam Pierce. And I'd like you to understand from the beginning that I had nothing to do with the shenanigans involved in bringing you here."

His voice had the low timbre of water flowing through woods, silky and cool. The *I don't want you here* was crystal clear, and totally confused her.

She focused sharply on the man as she strode forward to accept his hand. The lion was badly dressed. The mountain setting called for jeans; he was wearing gray flannel slacks and a starched white shirt and, for heaven's sake, a tie. His skin was too pale and the hollows under his eyes indicated a lack of sleep. None of that affected her first impression, but only accented it. This was a man of uncompromising drive, a man who would never be diverted by such innocuous entities as clothes, food, sunlight.

A fretful breeze brushed her skin when his hard grip enclosed her fingers. Two snakes could have shared a longer handshake. She felt his eyes skim over her mouth, her throat, her figure, and schooled her features into a deliberately sultry smile. "Sometime I'd like to tell you in detail what I think of those shenanigans. First, though, I'd appreciate hearing why I'm here," she said briskly.

"As soon as we get inside," he agreed. "And I want you to know that Harry or no Harry, you're under no obligation to stay."

"Fine." For a moment she was almost amused. He flanked her as she entered the cabin, keeping enough distance between them to insure they didn't accidentally breathe the same air. She'd never met a man who treated her like a leper before. Pierce couldn't know it, but for that instant she almost liked him.

After that, she was absorbed in her impressions of the place. At first glance, the rustic home had incredible potential for charm. A circular staircase led up to the second floor from the very center of the house. Natural textures of stone and glass and wood created a feeling of both space and privacy...if anyone looked hard enough beneath the clutter to see it.

The first room they walked into hadn't seen a woman's touch in a decade. The place smelled like old leather and wood, stale coffee and dust. Fat, low, rust-colored couches flanked a ceiling-to-floor stone fireplace; cluttered bookshelves lined the back walls, and tables were covered with debris—open books, forgotten coffee cups, chewed pencils, filled ashtrays. A man's shirt was strewn over a chair, and no one had thought to open a window to let in the day. There was no sign over the door that said Male Dominion, but there might as well have been.

The smallest frown etched itself between her brows. A little squalor didn't intimidate Leslie, except that the mess almost looked deliberately left for her to see. She felt increasingly disturbed as she looked around. There was no sign of a child or a teenager. Toys, tennies, hiking boots, records—nothing. The clutter all belonged to a grown man.

The man behind her cleared his throat. "I've been working here, Miss Stuart, twenty hours a day. So if you were expecting something like the Holiday Inn and maid service . . ."

She turned her head. "I wasn't expecting anything." Again she heard the unspoken resentment in his tone, and again she felt confused. He was the one who had set this up, not her. She'd expected an egotistical ass . . . but she'd also expected to be welcomed. If he didn't want her here, she couldn't imagine why she had been summoned.

"If you'll come this way—my office is set up on the second floor."

"Fine." She followed his lean frame to the circular stairway. "Where is he?"

Dark eyes swiveled around to pierce hers. "Where is who?"

"Or her?" She shook her head, trying for a smile. "The child I'm supposed to work with—where is he?"

His leonine brows arched up in a look of total perplexity. "You mean, Harry told you—"

"Harry didn't tell me anything, but it was obvious." She was growing impatient. "Look, Pierce, I'm tired of the games. For one thing, this whole traveling nonsense is ridiculous. Everything I need to work with a child is at home, in my school. If I'd known what was wrong with him, I could have at least brought some of my equipment. I don't know what on earth you expect me to accomplish in a short three weeks without the least idea of the child's background, his problems—"

"I have my doubts you can accomplish anything," he said wryly, "but as far as the tools of your trade, Miss Stuart, that won't be a problem. This will be your room." He motioned to the first door to the left as they reached the top of the stairs.

She glanced inside, and stilled. Someone had rather hastily and expensively assembled a feminine bedroom in French provincial and pale pink. The white carpeting looked new and the pink comforter on the twin bed still had a price tag hanging from it. Pink pillows, pink curtains, pink walls—the curtains had been hung man-style, missing most of the hooks, but that wasn't specifically what shocked her.

The bookshelves were filled with the exact texts she had in her office at home. The mobile blackboard adjusted to height, like the one she used every day at the school. The French provincial desk held her unusual choice of reading lamp, and the shelves in the corner contained the exact duplicates of her shelves at home, right down to the details of a Nerf ball and metronome.

"Satisfactory?" Pierce said dryly.

She shook her head. "I don't understand." Her tone was bewildered, and more than a little upset.

"Yes, well . . . you will in a moment."

He led the way to the next room, which was clearly his bedroom cum office. More coffee cups, more dust, more clutter, more darkness. Didn't the man ever open a curtain? A computer was on in the corner, its screen full of unintelligible numbers. Papers were stacked everywhere—he had to move things to find a place for her to sit.

As soon as she did he shoved a file in her hand. "I suggest you look at this first," he said quietly, immediately dropping into the swivel chair in front of the computer.

She glared furiously at him, but his attention was already claimed that quickly by the keyboard. He lit a cigarette, and she grimaced. The *last* thing this room needed was any more stale smoke.

Having no other choice, she opened the file and in minutes was absorbed by the material in front of her. Oculomotor dysfunctions, fixations, saccades, binocular vision therapy, amblyopia. When she finished the four typed pages, she sat back and drew her fingers together in a tent of concentration, not noticing or caring that the man had stopped playing with his machine and was staring at her.

"Well?"

Immediately she bristled. "Well, what?"

"Well, could you come to any conclusions from that particular report?" he demanded impatiently.

"Of course I can come to conclusions; it's my field," she said testily. "You've had the child see a proper eye doctor for diagnosis first, just as you should have. I would have ordered exactly these same tests. What you have is a child with a focusing difficulty and a little dyslexia. Though it's not uncommon, it's exactly the kind of learning disability that can go unnoticed for years—especially with a smart child. In simplest terms, he sees a whole page as a unit, but when he tries to read line by line—he simply can't."

Pierce's brooding eyes pinned hers. "So. Can you do something for him?"

"The dyslexia doesn't seem to be a major problem. Basically, dyslexia isn't 'curable,' but it's a condition that a child can be taught to overcome with time and patience. As far as the focusing difficulty—that's easily correctable with the proper kind of eye exercises."

"And you're familiar with the proper kind of eye exercises?"

"Look, Pierce." Leslie was thirsty, tired, mad and insulted. "You've spent an incredible amount of money to bring me out here, so I can't imagine why you're bothering to doubt my abilities now. I can tell you this: I can't turn the child around in three weeks, but I can make a darned good beginning. As far as I'm concerned, both you and Harry are welcome to go to hell. Now, either let me meet the child and start working with him or—"

"We've only got three weeks," he interrupted. "Can you or can't you make the person in that report able to read within a three-week period of time?"

If the tall lion weren't careful, Leslie would be tempted to show him what a five-foot-seven-inch woman could accomplish in a full-blown rage. "How on earth do you expect me to answer that without knowing the child? It depends on a thousand things—on what kind of person he is, how willing he is to cooperate with me, whether I can build up a rapport with him, how responsive he is to the exercises—I don't even know how old he is!"

"The child is prepared to put in twenty-hour days for the next three weeks and to do absolutely anything you say. To hell with rapport, and I can guarantee you full cooperation—"

"Dammit." Leslie vaulted to her feet and slammed the file on the counter. "I should have expected this. Children are not machines, buster. If you brought me here expecting me to treat a child like some computer—"

"This child is a machine, Leslie. He's also a living, breathing embarrassment to the government of this country. Shut up and sit down, would you?" He pushed back his hair in a gesture of total frustration and sighed.

"No way." Leslie was so incensed she was stuttering. "Anyone who thinks of a child as an embarrassment is a pompous, overgrown bastard as far as

I'm concerned. If the shoe fits, you *cretin*, wear it. I've never heard such an inhuman, cruel, insensitive—''

"The child, lady, is me." He glared at her. "I'm the one who can't read."

Two

You?" Leslie exclaimed.

"Yes. Me." Focusing on the rough paneled wall, Sam reached into his shirt pocket for a cigarette and scowled when he discovered the pack was empty. Five years ago, he'd completely quit smoking...and now he had managed to chain-smoke for the past three days waiting for this darn woman to get here.

The craving for nicotine was far worse now that he'd met her. She was the kind of woman who made a man worry that his fly was open. Even now, he could sense her eyes on him like the hot beam of a laser. The silence that followed grated on his nerves.

Leslie broke it. The crisp snap in her voice had vanished. If her instincts still warned her to be personally wary of the man, her professional curiosity reacted instantly to the challenge he represented. For at least a few moments, she didn't care if he were eight or ninety-eight. He couldn't read. "So, a great deal suddenly makes sense," she murmured thoughtfully. "There's no need to be embarrassed. I can't tell you how many adults in our society can't sound out the headlines in a newspaper," she added.

"I am *not* embarrassed," he snapped.

Oh, no? she thought wryly. The man shot off more sparks than a brushfire on a hot, dry day. She recognized the symptoms. Learning-disabled children were famous for earning the label Trouble. Belligerence, defensiveness, antisocial behavior—it always amazed Leslie to discover what lengths a child would go to to cover up his inability to read. Pierce, of the leonine brow and stubborn chin, was a little older than her usual delinquent—and not nearly as lovable—but he was the same brand of cookie.

The challenge of helping him rose in her like a flood. She tried to poke a mental finger in the dike. For a troubled kid she'd have stood on her head, but Pierce was distinctly a man—one with the power of private jets and bodyguards at his disposal, all to cover up his sensitivity about a little personal problem. Men with fragile egos made the most dangerous enemies. Leslie had paid her dues once on that score and didn't intend to pay them again.

She leaned back in the leather chair, crossed her legs and frowned at him. Leave, said her instincts. Her pulse made a terrific barometer when she was around the wrong kind of man. Her pulse had been tick-tick-ticking since she'd met him. "You don't really want me here," she said quietly.

"I never said that."

"You didn't have to." She motioned to the file. "But if you don't want to read, I can't imagine why you've gone to so much trouble to bring me here."

Sam finally found another pack of cigarettes in the third drawer of his desk. "I've gotten along just fine for thirty-four years without having to plod through Dick and Jane."

Lord, he was going to have to be handled with kid gloves. "So what is your field?"

"Mathematics."

"Well, that's the end of that conversation," Leslie said wryly. "I had to cheat to get through fifth-grade long division."

She won a startled smile. He had even, white teeth and a mouth that didn't look nearly as hard when he smiled. His eyes turned the silver-gray of wet stones in the sun. "You can't be serious."

"I'm perfectly serious. If you expected anyone with even a minimal knowledge of math, I can go right home."

"It isn't necessary," he said shortly.

Her tone turned immediately professional. "Fine. What is necessary?"

He shoveled a hand through his hair. "If you're not familiar with mathematics, I don't suppose you've ever heard of the Sherman Crown Award?"

"Nope."

"Well, it's an award given out annually to a mathematician who's contributed so-called special gifts in the field." He cleared his throat. "I happen to have come up with a formula..." He cleared his throat again. "The award's being given out in Rome this year—in August. And it happens to be the first time that the United States has won it in seven years."

"I take it you won it?"

"I never asked for it." He'd barely stubbed out one cigarette before he lit another. "I have to read a damn speech. Actually, if it were just that, I could memorize the thing, but the conference is really an international symposium to share work and ideas in my field. *If* I go, I have to be able to read. Papers will be exchanged, some of which have never been published before. It's information we need to know, that could be absolutely invaluable..." His voice broke off.

"You said 'if.' There's some question that you won't go?"

"*Someone* needs to go. The government keeps insisting that it's me." His tone was brittle with frustration. "My home base is Florida and they happen to pay my salary. My specialty is probabilistic risk assessment, an area that has long-term repercussions in the space program. They're pleased as punch I won this prize. At least they were, until they discovered—"

"That you couldn't read."

"They're scared as hell I'll embarrass them," he said wearily. "The country's so-called top mathematician couldn't master a second-grade primer if his life depended on it."

Leslie couldn't stand the smoke or darkness any longer. She pushed out of her chair. Jerking open the curtains, she threw open a window and let the crisp mountain air soothe the fragile feeling of tension building inside her.

She'd expected a child and didn't want a man. Especially not this man. In spite of herself—she knew better—she was beginning to feel empathy for him. Reading wasn't the issue. The problem was a man's pride and self-esteem and the label of being anyone's embarrassment.

No one could understand that better than Leslie. A label had been placed on her when she was sixteen and had crippled her life.

She turned. "You've made it a long way for a man with a reading problem."

"Reasonably." He couldn't take his eyes off her hair. The sun tangled silver in the loose waves when she shook her head.

"Fake modesty doesn't cut mustard with me, Sam. You've done far better than 'reasonably.'" She leaned back against the windowsill. "From reading that report, I know partly how you did it. You do read, obviously. You know the words, the vocabulary. You take in a page as a whole rather than line by line, which probably enabled you to get enough comprehension to trick half the world when you were in school." She hesitated. "Still. No matter how tricky you were—and believe me, I've run into some tricky kids in my time—I really don't see how someone didn't catch up with you long before this. And mathematics—you must have had to read problems."

"Not in the usual way kids read problems. Not in the schools I attended."

"No?"

"No."

It was like prying teeth. "So what kind of school did you go to?" she asked patiently.

"One where they taught me geometry when I was four, and no one gave a damn whether I could conquer Dickens as long as I had calculus mastered at ten."

She understood immediately that he'd been to a school for the gifted...and that he'd admit that aloud when he was six feet under. Amused, she was tempted to go over and shake him. Pierce clearly hated every minute of this interview. His hands were half clenched, his shoulder muscles were bunched inside his shirt and he looked ready to vault out of his chair at the first excuse. Lions didn't like to show weakness, and those searing dark eyes were wary.

"Where I went to school is hardly your problem," he said curtly. "All that matters is whether you can teach a grown man to read in three weeks. If you don't want to be involved, that's fine by me, too. I'll have a plane here to pick you up by tomorrow morning if you want to leave."

She hesitated. Professionally, she was itching to get him into the other room where she could verify the diagnosis of the tests in his file. Emotionally, though, she wanted that plane. She very much didn't want to be involved.

You're one of those men who have to be strong all the time, aren't you, Sam? she thought. A man just doesn't show weakness to a woman. It's driving you nuts that I'm even here...

An old memory twisted like a headache in her temples. The boy could even have been a sixteen-year-old Pierce. Johnny had had sandy hair and sexy dark eyes; he'd been all lean muscle, he'd had a beautiful mouth. Leslie had also been sixteen at that time, and no one could have convinced her there was anything dangerous about Johnny. He'd brought her a yellow carnation and arrived at her house in a battered old pickup to take her to the junior prom.

He was just a proud boy trying very hard to be a man, and a man to Johnny was someone who was always strong and powerful and macho. When a small problem had come up, he hadn't been able to own up to it honestly because it would have dented that fragile male ego. And because Johnny had to be a man, Leslie had ended up thrown out of Rawlings, a little town in upper Minnesota, at the ripe age of sixteen.

"Well?" Sam said impatiently.

Leslie smiled. "Oh, I'll take you on," she said gently. "Believe me, I'll take you on, Pierce—as long as we can agree to terms. For three weeks, I'm the boss. For the next three weeks, you live by my rules. Understand?"

Harry quietly rapped on the bedroom door and then stepped inside the darkened room. "Pierce?" he hissed.

Sam's eyes snapped awake. "What's wrong?"

"That woman, that's what's wrong. She's been up for two hours—"

"What time is it?"

"Not even eight o'clock in the morning," Harry grumbled.

Sam stared at him, then groggily climbed out of bed and searched for his pants. He'd worked late, and his mouth had a stale taste. He'd smoked too many cigarettes the night before, and topped that off with a straight Scotch that was doing nothing for his headache this morning. "So what's so terrible?" he said impatiently.

"She was up before six, wreaking havoc and dressed like..." Harry rolled his eyes and flushed. "She's got every window in the place open downstairs. It's freezing—"

"So she's a fresh-air nut," Sam said placidly.

"She's got two bags of food by the back door that she expects me to throw out. And she's made out this ridiculous shopping list—"

"Harry, we've got to cater to the lady for the next three weeks. What is she, a vegetarian?" He zipped up his pants, reached for socks and sat on the bed again. "It figures, but it doesn't matter. Just do what she says and relax."

"I told her I was supposed to do the cooking and housekeeping for you two, and sort of act like, you know, a chaperon." He flushed again. "She started laughing, and said she'd help with the first two because I'd have my hands full with the last. She said she hadn't been without sex for a full three weeks in years and didn't intend to start now. Then she asked me if I were *married*!"

Sam smothered a grin. "And what did you say?" he asked gravely.

"What did I say? I said nothing! I came up here. Listen," he said heatedly. "I'm telling you that woman is no schoolteacher like I ever met. If you ask me—"

"If you ask me the lady's got you so tied around her fingers you can't think straight, Harry. Calm down."

Harry huffed. "We'll see how you calm down when you see what she's wearing. And she's thrown out every liquor bottle in the place, and all your cigarettes were burned up in the fireplace this morning.''

At that, Sam felt a nicotine fit coming on. His eyes whisked over the room, searching for his last pack...and a clean shirt. "Relax," he advised again. "Give me a minute and I'll get downstairs."

"You'd better hurry. I'm telling you a man isn't safe in a room alone with her. When I came down the stairs this morning, she kissed me on the cheek! Just walked up bold as you please—"

"Harry," said the sweet reproachful voice from behind him. Harry froze. "I was just trying to wish you a good morning. I thought you liked it. You certainly said—"

"I never did. I never said anything. I swear it." Sick eyes focused helplessly on Sam.

Sam's eyes were focused on the potent baggage behind him. If he had a linear problem focusing, he had no problem taking in the total package. Leslie was all legs. Her white shorts couldn't get any tighter over her exquisitely tight fanny. Above that she wore a loose, billowy yellow blouse that might have been modest if she'd buttoned the buttons. When she whipped up Sam's window shades, morning sun lavished warmth on her satin-white cleavage. Above that, her hairstyle was a froth of pale gold. Her sulky mouth had been glossed, and the barest hint of mascara darkened the sexy promises in her eyes.

She was a walking breathing danger to a man's blood pressure. He met her sultry brown eyes squarely. The clang of challenge meeting challenge could have been heard in the next county.

"We need to get to work," she informed him.

He smiled deliberately and stood up. Somewhere in the room was a clean shirt. If she'd get out of his vision, he could probably find it. "If I'd known you wanted to start this early, I would already have been up. I assumed you'd be tired after traveling."

She shook her head, and then concentrated a distinctly loving glance on Harry. "Come on," she said sweetly. "You and I can go downstairs and fix breakfast . . . together."

"Pierce probably has stuff he needs me to do—" Harry sent him a hopeful glance.

"You go ahead," Sam said smoothly.

"I can fix breakfast alone for all of us. You don't have to help. You can just go on into the living room and . . . read or something. You like to read. That's your business, isn't it?" Harry said as they walked down the stairs. His tone was that of a desperate man.

Sam swallowed a chuckle, but his smile had long faded by the time he'd grabbed a shirt and headed for the bathroom. Once the door was locked and he had a razor in his hand, he admitted to the mirror in total privacy that the woman shook him.

There hadn't been a woman in a long time who had turned him on with a simple look at her. Leslie sent his blood pressure to stroke level and Sam knew what to do with a woman like her like a toddler knew what to do with an uncaged tigress.

He'd had women in his life. As a kid he'd been labeled a prodigy—he'd hated that name then and he hated it now. Regardless, when he was of an age, he'd made love to his first female counterpart—another prodigy, a girl possibly more brilliant than he. Since then, his world had been limited to intellectuals. Eggheads were as lonely as everyone else; he'd never lacked for female companionship. He'd just had high hopes of finding a woman who wanted to talk something besides quantum theory after making love.

The frustration had been building inside him for months, maybe years. Sex wasn't the issue; life was. At thirty-four, he was increasingly conscious that he was missing the whole mainstream of existence. To take a walk in the rain—he never had. To meet normal people—he'd never had the chance. From the time he was four his parents had known he was gifted. He'd been pushed, cosseted, cushioned, protected and steered into a specialized environment where he could use and challenge his intellect. His brain was everything; emotions were always conveniently shelved as if they didn't exist. Only, when the hell did a man get a chance to just live?

He'd thought the crowning blow had happened with his last boss. Malek had taken him aside and tactfully informed him that he would provide Sam with a woman whenever he felt it was necessary. Sex was obviously a function necessary to keep the brain machine happy and healthy.

That wasn't, Sam had discovered yesterday, the crowning blow. Leslie was. He'd initially and privately labeled her a bossy bitch, and she hadn't done a thing to make him change that label...but that didn't matter. She was a sensual earth queen, a sexual temptress, a primitive Lorelei. She was the life and freedom he'd never had, the sex he'd always wanted, the sensuality he'd missed and hadn't the least idea how to express in himself. She was warmth—no, he corrected himself fleetingly—she was heat.

Having to admit his problem to her the day before had been painful. Coexisting with her for the next three weeks struck him as a very bad idea for a man with any pride. Sam already had a small problem with pride. Still, the moment he stepped downstairs he felt his sense of humor returning.

Harry was sitting at the kitchen table with that sick flush on his cheeks. His hair was wet-combed and looked neater than Sam had ever seen it. His shirt was neatly tucked in. Harry never bothered to tuck in his shirt. He was eating scrambled eggs, and Harry hated eggs.

One woman had reduced the gruff old coot to Silly Putty. Sam was amused.

"Eggs," Leslie said lightly as she set a plate in front of Sam. "Toast—it'll be whole wheat tomorrow. Orange juice and no coffee—as of tomorrow we'll have herbal teas. After Harry goes shopping for me. Right, Harry?''

Harry couldn't nod fast enough.

"No more caffeine in this house. Not for the next three weeks. We need energy foods for the regimen Pierce needs to go through."

She glanced at him, waiting, but Sam said nothing. She was full of horse manure, bossier than any woman he'd ever met, and clearly dying for a man to challenge her. It wasn't going to be him. "As I told you," he said quietly, "you're the boss for the next three weeks." He paused. "As long as I see you're doing what you're paid to do."

"You'll read," she said sweetly. "Believe me, Pierce, I'll have you quoting from *Little Women* inside three weeks."

Harry choked. Leslie thumped him gently on the back, and winked at Pierce.

Two hours later, they were upstairs in her bedroom-office, and Sam found himself increasingly curious about the chameleon the lady had turned into. Get the woman anywhere near the tools of her trade and she forgot the sloe-eyed looks, the smiles to disturb a man's breathing, the come-hither posture.

For the past hour she'd run him through a series of tests, leaving him in no doubt that she knew her business. More than that, she was a completely different Leslie when she was working. She'd snapped a pair of oversize eyeglasses on her nose. Her voice had become impossibly gentle. She'd coaxed him through the tedious tests that should have embarrassed him. Dammit, he stumbled over every third word like a second-grade failure, but somehow he hadn't been embarrassed.

Sometime during the past hour, she'd bitten off her lip gloss and dragged a hand carelessly through her hair. She was pacing at the moment, a puckish frown marring her brow. The glasses had been thrown on the bed and a pencil was jammed behind her ear.

He had the inclination to ask the real Leslie Stuart to please stand up. Either the temptress or the professional was real. Both of them couldn't be. The question disturbed him enough that he almost missed what she was saying.

"All right. You had excellent people do your initial testing, Pierce, but before we start work, do you mind telling me why John Brooks is the name at the top of that file?"

"I thought that would have been obvious. The State Department wasn't in a hurry to let it be known that their top mathematician couldn't read."

"Hmm." Leslie turned to the adjustable blackboard and tugged it to the center of the room. She sent a studying glance to Sam, then started flipping the screws to change the board's height. For two solid hours, her mind had been absorbed with methods of tackling his unique set of problems. She was itching to get at him the way a mosquito craved blood. She *knew* she could help him.

Other, more emotional considerations were only gradually starting to nag her. "I still don't understand how or why the government happened to pick me," she said casually. "There are thousands of reading therapists in this country with a little opthalmological training to back that."

"Do you want help with that blackboard?"

"No."

"Well, in answer to your question—the government didn't pick you. I did."

Her brows shot up. "I beg your pardon?"

He dropped into a chair, unable to stop watching her. Her shorts had ridden up when she bent to adjust the blackboard. Her legs were a sun-kissed gold, and where there should have been a tan line at the crease of her leg and fanny...there wasn't. He guessed she was gold all over—a thought that was enough to arouse him like a teenage boy at a drive-in. "Months ago, I caught an article about you in a scholastic magazine," he said absentmindedly. "The piece was on how regular school systems were failing our children—I gather you feel rather strongly about the subject?"

"You bet I do!"

A slash of a smile curved his mouth. "Anyway, that article cited examples of how fast you'd turned older teenagers and adults around who initially couldn't read a word." He shrugged. "I suggested your name to the appropriate people. Naturally, they did a little more checking than that before—''

Suddenly her palms were growing damp and a sick feeling invaded the pit of her stomach. "What kind of checking?" she asked lightly.

He hesitated, catching that sudden glint of fire in her eyes—anger? For the oddest moment, he thought it was fear, which made no sense. "Leslie, it would never have been my choice to pry into your private life," he said quietly.

She had to stop her hands from trying to clench into fists. "You've seen whatever file they put together, haven't you?"

He nodded silently. He saw no reason to lie to her. Truthfully, he would have been equally annoyed to have a stranger fumbling through his vital statistics. But Leslie was clearly more than annoyed. Her face had turned pale and her eyes were an amber blaze. An invasion of privacy was one thing, but he'd read that file, and she could surely guess what was in it. There was nothing that should have so strongly upset her. His tone was carefully light, almost teasing. "You got a traffic ticket when you were eighteen. You vote Republican. You worked your way through college; you were a straight-A student."

When she said nothing, he continued gently, "Look. All they really wanted to know was whether you were into politics, or whether you associated with people who were political subversives. That may not be forgivable, but I think you can understand where they were coming from."

"In other words, they checked out in detail every man I've slept with over the years." She hissed fiercely, "A hell of a long list, wasn't it, Pierce?"

He thought fleetingly that a flood, or an earthquake, might be convenient at that particular moment. Only no natural disaster appeared to be forthcoming, which left him in embarrassingly hot water. He loosened the collar of his shirt. "No one was trying to make a judgment on your private life. And besides, you're an attractive woman. Obviously you've had men in your life—"

"Dozens," she snapped.

He tried humor. "At least none of them were political activists."

"I would appreciate knowing how many years that report covered."

"Since you were an adult. Obviously what you did as a kid had no possible relevance—"

"What exact age did the report begin with?"

She really would have thrived during the Inquisition. "I think—eighteen."

To his total shock, she suddenly relaxed. The brittleness faded from her expression, her color returned. Her chin tilted up and he caught the flash of the other Leslie—the one who flaunted perfect, firm breasts with a certain posture, the one with the defiant dark eyes that made a man think of she-cats, the one with the full red mouth that a man couldn't conceivably stop staring at. The room was charged with sexual electricity so fast that the voltage threatened a power overload.

Her sudden short laugh was smoke-edged, dangerous. "Funny, isn't it?"

At the moment he couldn't see anything remotely humorous. "What is?"

"That I so easily passed the government's little test on whether or not I was suitably trustworthy. Character is a very funny word, Pierce. Not too many years ago, a woman's character would have been severely in question if she'd done the least bit of fooling around. Now, no one cares if I slept with the army and threw in the marines." She drawled blithely, "I've come damn close to doing both and never did care who knew it."

She picked up a piece of chalk and discovered, to her fury, that her fingers were trembling. Stupid. It was utterly stupid to be so upset. Salt stung her eyes; she blinked furiously. The government was incredibly dense. Her life was full of men; the idiots had assumed that meant she slept around. If she had any sense, she'd be laughing. That was exactly what she wanted them to think, the world to think, Pierce to think. She'd discovered a long time ago that men rarely challenged a sexually aggressive woman. She'd learned how to flaunt the label years ago. As far as she was concerned, the whole damn world could think she was as loose as a goose.

Only there was a tiny incident in her past that she wanted no one to know about, a secret she'd worked for years to bury deeply. And that little character report came just a little too close to discovering it. The old, terrible anxiety ached in her stomach like one ice-white slash of remembered shame.

She suddenly whirled on Pierce. Heat rushed to her cheeks when she realized how long he'd been utterly still, watching her, those leonine brows drawn together in arched perplexity. And contempt? For a lady who made it no secret that she was promiscuous?

"Ready to work?" She meant her tone to sound brisk and businesslike. Instead, she knew darn well it sounded hollow.

Sam wasn't the least bit ready to work. He had the sudden horrible instinct that the lady glaring at him by the blackboard was close to tears.

Three

___

Look, I never meant to upset you," Sam said hesitantly. He knew nothing of women like her. Actually, he was unsure how to soothe *any* woman in emotional distress, and he felt as awkward as an overgrown bear cub as he quietly moved behind her. With more instinct than sense he touched her hair, then let his hand drop to her shoulder.

"Leslie, we're not on some battlefield here. I never wanted to be your enemy," he said slowly. "That report was about an unusual woman. A lady who worked herself through school. That couldn't have been easy. A lady who battled a city school system to put together her own educational program. A lady who's already been written up in national magazines for her successes." He paused, starkly aware of how rigidly she was standing, how sweet her perfume was. "There isn't anything in there that you shouldn't be extraordinarily proud of—but I can understand you resent anyone prying into your life. If it matters that much to you, I can have the report destroyed."

Leslie closed her eyes and felt the rash urge to turn, wrap her arms around him and simply be held as she hadn't been held in years. The hand quietly kneading her shoulder, his liquid voice, the tickling sensation of his fingers in her hair . . . these were what her instincts had warned her to be wary of from the minute she'd met Sam. Now she knew why. She could feel magic she didn't want to feel, promises in his touch that couldn't be real, need that started in the curl of her toes and threatened to flood her.

Sexual vibrations came with life; they didn't matter. She could control sexual feelings, but other emotions were much harder to rule. A strong man had needed to spill his vulnerability in front of her yesterday. How could she not feel empathy, the urge to care and share? They were both loners; they had both suffered labels. A current could pass between a man and a woman so fast.

But not for her, and never with this man. She heard the echo of what he'd said: *nothing you shouldn't be extraordinarily proud of*. He didn't know—no one would ever know—that she'd done things for which she was extraordinarily ashamed.

Sam wouldn't be in such an all-fired hurry to touch her if he knew what kind of woman she really was.

She swallowed hard, opened her eyes on the blank blackboard in front of her and stepped away from his hands.

"Leslie—"

"Forget it," she said swiftly. "My life's an open book. For all I care, the government can publish that whole file in the *New York Times*. I don't know where you got the idea I was upset. The only thing upsetting me right now is that we're wasting time."

She felt his dark eyes boring into her back and thought, Put him off, Stuart. Do it now and do it fast and make damn sure he never gets that close again.

She drew one small circle in the middle of the blackboard, then two more on each side of that. "Now." Her tone was brisk, pleasant, efficient. She flashed him a quick smile. "If you're ten, this first exercise is as much fun as alphabet soup. Unfortunately, Pierce, you're going to hate it. Would you step up here, please, and touch your nose to the middle circle."

He stared at her. "Touch my—"

"Yes, you heard me. If you'll bring me a Bible, I'll swear this works and isn't just something I conjured up to make a grown man look foolish." She handed him two bits of chalk. "Once your nose is pressed to the center circle, use the chalk to start making clockwise circles on the blackboard—here and here—

and make them as small and perfectly round as you know how."

With his nose jammed to the board, he made her damned circles—clockwise, then counterclockwise. He said absolutely nothing, primarily because his jaws were jammed together. The moment before might never have been. She had the gift of changing from vulnerable angel to witch. Bitch, Pierce mentally corrected.

So, Leslie thought wryly, the lion didn't like to make circles, but she'd certainly managed to turn him off. That stupid moment was over, her pulse was back to normal, her brain fully functioning again. Work was the key.

"Done," she said briskly at the end of ten minutes.

Sam stepped back from the blackboard and flushed bright red when he saw his so-called circles. A kindergartner could have done better in his sleep. Expecting a snappy comment from Leslie, he got instead a gentle "That's the point, Pierce. Balance is related to focus. We'll get you there. Now sit—" she glanced around "—on the bed."

He sat on the edge of her bed. She drew a chair closer to him and perched on it, leaning closer. Her scent—a sweet faint musk, the warmth of woman—assaulted him. When she bent over, he could not only see her cleavage but the clear outline of both full, firm breasts. The tips strained against the cotton fabric when she bunched both hands into fists.

"Now listen," she said firmly. "I'm going to open a hand at random, and the instant you see my hand open, I want you to slap it. Concentrate, Pierce. You've got to watch both of my hands at the same time."

He watched, slapped, watched, slapped. "Faster now," she encouraged. "I'm going to spread my hands farther apart this time. Watch both hands..."

Beads of perspiration formed on his brow before fifteen minutes had passed. Three weeks of this just wasn't going to work. He'd never bargained on physical games. He couldn't take his eyes off her breasts and the only thing he was concentrating on was the ache in his groin and an invasive curiosity about what made Leslie tick.

"Look, why aren't we *reading* something?" he demanded finally.

"Because you're not ready to read, sweets, that's why. Come on. Again. You're going to get a heck of a lot faster than this before we go on to the next exercise, I guarantee it."

She worked with him for two hours, doing the most confoundedly childish exercises he'd ever seen in his life. Harry came in once to see if they wanted a cup of coffee. Leslie gently, firmly closed the door in his face. When the lady was working, she was working. Only her idea of work was drastically different from his.

They played catch with a Nerf ball like toddlers. Then she put masking tape on the carpet and made him walk lines, sometimes with one eye closed, sometimes with the other. She put him counting strokes on the metronome. At the end of two hours, he was coldly furious.

Leslie was extraordinarily pleased. "You're doing fine," she said warmly, and glanced at the slim gold watch on her wrist. "Lunchtime. And after lunch..." Her eyes dawdled over him, stem to stern. "Do you have a pair of jeans, Pierce?"

"Jeans?"

"Jeans. Denims. You've heard the term?"

"Of course I've heard the term, and yes, I've obviously got a pair of jeans, but—"

"Fine, after lunch, put on jeans. And by any remote chance, do you have hiking boots? Because after lunch, we're working outside. There are certain exercises I can put you through a thousand times better in a natural environment, where we've got lots of space."

Frustration bunched inside him like a cold fist in his stomach. His dark eyes seared hers. He saw the beautiful red mouth, the natural, sensual toss of silver-gold hair, the brilliantly cold brown eyes. There was no hint of the vulnerable woman he'd seen earlier. Every instinct told him he was being paid back in spades for having had a glimpse of that vulnerability; but there was a limit to how long he was willing to pay that price.

"You don't have a problem with that program, do you, Pierce?" she said sweetly. "You said you didn't mind working twenty-hour days if it would help."

"I don't."

"If you don't like my teaching methods, I'll be glad to go. As I recall, you agreed that I was the boss for the next three weeks."

He stood up, rather slowly. She wanted to leave. That was exactly what this was about. She wanted him to give her the first excuse to take a plane out of here. All at once, Sam could hardly wait to find out just how far and how hard she was going to try to push him. "I'll meet you downstairs," he said shortly.

She met him outside the door at one o'clock, and could see at a glance he hadn't gotten over his little stew. Some men had a terrible problem taking orders from a woman. Pierce clearly didn't trust her, and that didn't help matters any.

Of course, he was right not to trust her. He was finished with exercises for the day, though she wasn't about to tell him that. Eyes could only take so much stress; to push too far too fast was inviting a step backward. Leslie knew exactly what she was doing, and at the moment her goal was exposing the man to a little sun and recreation.

In fact, Pierce was about to be exposed to a lot of things over the next three weeks. Sam was going to learn to read. He was also going to give up cigarettes, take up exercise and normal living hours, eat proper foods. And if he didn't like it, he could order the Cessna back to the airstrip to take her home.

Ever since this morning, she'd desperately wanted to go home.

The Sam in front of her wearing jeans and hiking boots wasn't helping. The jeans were worn to a blue-white and accented his muscular legs. In sunshine, he cast too darn big a shadow and his dark eyes leveled on hers, a man's eyes that swiveled over her bare legs, the open throat of her blouse, her mouth... She licked suddenly-dry lips. It was getting worse, this ridiculous feeling of shakiness when she was around him. It had to stop.

She shook her head at him, cocked a challenging brow. "You must have misunderstood—I told you jeans and boots. No shirt, Pierce—off it goes."

Expecting mutiny—daring him to mutiny—she watched his hands immediately and obediently reach for his shirt buttons. "I'm also wearing underwear. You want those off, too?" he asked smoothly.

His slash of a smile startled her. She said calmly, "Maybe later."

"Whatever you consider necessary...to reading therapy."

"Yes." He dropped his shirt on the porch steps. His chest was tight and sinewy. Long golden hairs sprawled around his ribs and abdomen and she caught herself staring...and then quickly turning away. "This way," she called over her shoulder.

"I suppose I would be breaking one of your rules if I asked you where we were going?"

"Where we're going is not your problem, Pierce. Orange is. Finding natural things that are orange and focusing on them. Most people see the obvious colors in nature—greens and browns and the blue of the sky. Orange is rare, but there's plenty of it. You'll just have to look hard. Concentrate on focusing now."

He concentrated on the twitch of her fanny as she walked, her lithe, feminine stride, the bounce of her hair that was silver in sun, gold in shade.

Leslie hiked down the ravine, then up again, then through a stand of thick Douglas firs. She reveled in the sweet pines, a hot baking sun, the clear air and craggy mountain peaks. Alone, she would have enjoyed the walk, but she was not alone and the hike was not for enjoyment. A half hour passed before she glanced back, and noted with satisfaction the sheen of perspiration pearled on Sam's forehead. "You haven't seen one orange thing yet?"

"The wing of an oriole. Some kind of wildflower. I didn't realize you wanted an accounting."

"I do," she said gravely. "I want to hear about every single orange thing you find."

After that he concentrated harder on her rump—specifically on that exact perfect curve where the lady so badly needed a slap. Both palms itched to give it to her. He wasn't fussy which one did the honors.

She was part mountain goat. She scrambled up slopes and over rocks, whisked around trees and found time to raise her face to the sun when he was damn hard-pressed to keep up with her—partly because his attention was on her instead of walking, and partly because he'd spent the past three months closeted on a project that had left him no time for exercise.

"You're not getting tired, are you?" she called over her shoulder.

"No." The taunt in her voice was unmistakable. Never mind that his left hamstring was killing him and he could feel a blister forming on his right foot.

"Because if you're tired—"

"I said no."

"You're not doing very well with orange. Maybe you'd better start looking for purple."

"Whatever you say, honey."

Her vertebrae stiffened with that "honey." Sam grinned and then raised his eyes skyward. Lord only knew how long she'd make him pay for that one.

"Anyone heard the one about the traveling salesman?"

When that got no response, Harry tried, "Found the best fishing spot you've ever seen this afternoon. Mountain trout big as a yardstick and too fat to fit in a frying pan."

When that got no response, he tried, "Anyone want more potatoes?"

Pierce wanted more potatoes. Once the bowl was passed and set down again, the atmosphere at the dinner table again resembled a cross between a pending blizzard and the heat of an electric storm. Perplexed, Harry stole uneasy glances at both of them.

Leslie was wearing a black top cut low enough to make a man's eyes sizzle, and was pushing a fork around the meat loaf he'd made just for her. It was exactly what he'd caught her doing the last time he'd looked at her. Not that she didn't make him damned nervous when she smiled at him, but he'd sort of counted on one of those smiles when she'd come down to dinner. He'd gotten no smiles and no conversation.

Pierce had shown up for dinner freshly showered, shirtless and barefoot. He was eating like a man threatened with starvation, but he wasn't talking much. Harry only had to look at him to wince. Pierce's shoulders were the color of a hot brick and his chest was the shade of fire embers.

"Well, now—" Harry cleared his throat. He didn't have the least idea what was wrong with the two of them, but the dead silence was driving him nuts. "I guess I expected you two to work all day in the office. Never heard of any reading lessons being taught outside."

"The lady knows her business, Harry," Sam immediately defended her.

"I'm sure she does, I'm sure she does." Harry cleared his throat again. "So, everything's going hunky-dory? Just a peaceful three weeks ahead for the three of us—"

He heard the clatter of fork against plate, and glanced at Leslie. Her face was white and she looked distinctly ill. "Something wrong with my meat loaf?" he said with alarm.

Leslie rapidly stood up and dropped the napkin by her plate. With a faint smile she bent down and dropped a kiss on Harry's temple. "Your meat loaf is perfectly delicious and you're an absolute sweetheart, Harry, but if you'll both please excuse me..."

Harry stared at Sam when she was gone. "Something I said?"

Sam shook his head, pushed back his plate and automatically reached back on the counter for his cigarettes and lighter. They'd disappeared.

"You saw her kiss me. That was twice now. I'm telling you she's not like any schoolteacher I ever had, not by a long shot." He grimaced at Pierce. "I hid one pack for you in the far drawer by the sink under the tin foil. And now that she's gone, we can pour out this milk—I've got a bottle of Scotch in my room. One shot or two?"

"None for me, but thanks, Harry." He was too busy casting a speculative glance at the stairs.

By nine o'clock Leslie was busy wearing out a strip of her bedroom carpet. Sam was upstairs too; she'd heard his step fifteen minutes before. Since then, her hands had been jammed in the front pockets of her white jeans and she hadn't stopped pacing. She wasn't sure which she felt more: ashamed or guilty. Granted, Pierce had been hostile that first day, but it had to do with his reading. From then on, he'd been nothing but kind and considerate with her. She'd been the shrew.

Dammit, he hadn't snapped at her once on the entire three-hour hike. It just wasn't natural for a man to be so darned . . . *gentle*.

Frowning, she stopped pacing long enough to open a drawer and rummage in her cosmetic bag for a small plastic bottle. Closing her fist around it, she took another swing around the room. Finally, she glared at the door as if it were a demon and turned the knob.

Downstairs she could hear a newspaper rustling in the living room—Harry was reading. She tiptoed out in the hall on bare feet, stood like a statue in front of Sam's closed door, and felt an imaginary cotton wad block her throat.

The night had turned cool, but every inch of her skin felt oddly hot and her palms were ridiculously clammy. She knocked so softly a mouse couldn't have heard it, and felt doomed when Sam immediately called out, "It's not locked—just push it open."

She did. A small reading lamp was on between his desk and bed, illuminating a freshly showered Pierce wearing a towel. Perched at the bottom of the bed, he was leaning over, applying first-aid cream to a blister on his right heel. The sight of the blister combined with the look of his red shoulders and chest made her feel violently ill.

If she'd looked just a few inches higher, she might have seen Sam's mouth curve, his dark eyes flash satisfaction, but she never took her eyes off his chest. "I came to bring you something. Aloe. It'll take the sting out of that sunburn."

He screwed the top back on the first-aid cream tube and tossed it on his desk. "Thanks," he said shortly.

It wouldn't wait any longer to get out. "Sam, I'm sorry." She gulped. "Really sorry."

"Why?" he asked dryly. "I think you did exactly what you wanted to do."

"No." She shook her head. "No. I honestly didn't realize how long we were in the sun. I would never have forced you on that long a hike if I'd known."

"Can I have that bottle you brought?" When she handed it to him, he studied her. Where his flesh was red, hers had simply gained another layer of honey gold, and the slash of apricot glow on her cheeks accented her fragile bones. Her skin could make satin look rough.

"You didn't force me to do anything," he assured her. "I can't tell you how many years it's been since I've had an entire afternoon to spend on nothing but getting a good sunburn. I wanted it—the sun and the exercise." He opened her bottle and tipped a little of the creamy liquid into his palm. He spread it on his chest, watching Leslie watch him. It seemed to bother her. He was discovering that he enjoyed very much bothering Leslie. "And then, you said that hike was important for focusing, didn't you?"

He watched her chew the small word around in her mouth before she could spit out the lie. "Yes."

"So you have nothing to feel badly about. Help?"

For an instant she couldn't fathom what he meant by "help," but then he turned his back to her and raised her plastic container so she could see it. There wasn't a chance on earth she was going to smooth that cream on his bare back.

Only there didn't seem to be anyone else volunteering, and she was certainly the one responsible for his sunburn. Lips compressed, she moved forward and snatched the bottle from his hand. The fragrant cream felt warm in her palms. She hesitated and then, gently, carefully, applied it to the slope of his shoulders.

Sam immediately let out a sound, and she stopped. "Did I hurt you?"

"No."

His skin was so hot. And smooth. Her fingertips fluttered over his flesh, anxious not to hurt him, just to soothe in the cream. His skin absorbed it as fast as she applied it. A bead of perspiration trickled between her breasts. She had to pour out more cream on her palms.

Her pulse informed her she felt as safe as rotting timbers in an earthquake. She simply didn't do things like this. She didn't seek men out at night, didn't enter their bedrooms, didn't touch them when they were all but naked. Still, Sam so obviously wasn't like other men. He'd led a sheltered life, he was gentle; and she'd steamrollered him into that horrible long hike that now left her feeling confused and guilty. She'd so badly misjudged him. She'd been afraid he was a lion and taken out her own fears and frustrations on a lamb.

"Does it feel too cold?" she asked briskly.

"It feels . . . incredibly good."

"I'll be done in a minute."

"Don't hurry."

A wisp of a smile appeared on her lips. "Don't tell me the mathematician's a closet hedonist, Sam?"

"This mathematician is wondering if you hire out on the side to do backrubs."

"No." She finished his shoulder blades, moved down to the small of his back and felt her blood pulse in her veins. The towel wrapped around his waist had tugged loose because of the way he was sitting. The red line of sunburn demarked acceptable touch territory from forbidden areas. She really didn't want to get near either.

She really wanted to be back in Minnesota. "Pierce?"

"Hmm?"

As fast as possible, she replaced the top on the bottle and stepped away from him. "I'm qualified to teach you, but now that I've seen your diagnostic tests, I think you need to understand that I'm not the most qualified. In fact, there's a teacher in Atlanta, a really nice woman, who—"

"I have no problem with your qualifications." Sam turned, dark eyes pinning her as he stood up. She was as unnerved as he'd seen her this morning, but in a completely different way. This morning she'd looked haunted, frightened somehow; her eyes had been sick with it, her face white with whatever had upset her. Now she was trying hard not to look at him and the flush on her cheeks went beyond an afternoon in the sun. That flush had him mesmerized. Watching her fingers tangle together made him smile. The temptress nervous? Because she'd delivered a little backrub? He couldn't fathom it.

"I'm content with the arrangement we have," he said slowly. "Unless you're not. A man, Leslie?"

"Pardon?"

"At home. These three weeks must have cut into your private life, maybe made a relationship awkward for you? I don't know or care what Harry told you—but you're welcome to call anyone you want to from here." He added conversationally, "What's his name?"

She paused and then said smoothly, "Actually, there isn't one man, but two. And that is kind of the point—I have to admit that being here does make things a little awkward for me. Harry didn't give me a chance to do much of anything but close up the house. I had personal plans, private plans...."

Juggling two men in bed, she would have him believe. Sam certainly wouldn't have doubted it—if she weren't twisting her fingers into knots. She's lying, he thought. Why? "Either one of them a serious relationship?"

"Both."

He nodded. "The phone's right there. I can go downstairs while you..."

She shook her head swiftly, and edged toward the door. "No, I don't really need to call." She added, "Not right now. Tomorrow." She'd nearly made it to the door when he was there, standing in front of her. She hadn't seen him move. Remember what a lamb he is, she reminded herself. But he suddenly didn't seem like such a lamb, and the sensation of being stalked whispered through her senses like a warning, like hyperawareness, like danger. The tawny hair on his chest was glistening with aloe, scented with the sweet herb. The breadth of his shoulders was twice hers. The towel hung too low on his hips, and he was simply far too close.

"Tomorrow you can call your friends," he agreed. "And in the meantime I owe you a thank-you for your cream."

"That's not necessa—"

He promised her, "This won't take anything away from your men. They couldn't possibly mind."

He guessed it was a mistake and didn't care. He guessed he was risking an unbearable day tomorrow; as a man he didn't want her to know he probably didn't have half of her sexual experience, and he'd won the apology from her—all of that should have been enough. Only it wasn't enough. He'd wanted her the instant he met her. She was the tease of emotional life he'd never had, the temptation of earth and sun and sex at its most primitive. Sex was out of the question, but a stolen kiss he was definitely going to take.

She saw his mouth coming closer and thought of a dozen ways to stop him. The right word would have done it. Laughter often worked, and physically she knew enough self-defense to insure no man came anywhere near her. She could have done a dozen things, two dozen...and she didn't. She felt his breath—warm, sweet. His eyes were a lazy, fathomless gray black, his lashes short and thick. And then his lips touched hers.

She closed her eyes, still as a cat in the sun. If his arms had reached out to hold her or if she'd sensed the least sexually aggressive move on his part, she knew she could have broken free. Nothing touched but lips. His mouth was warm on hers, soothing, coaxing. There was no pressure. The kiss came and then went again, teasing her, haunting her...

The tip of his tongue traced her lower lip, and still he made no move to press or push for more than the gentle caress. His chest was less than inches from hers. In less than a second he could have surrounded her; she didn't understand why his arms didn't move up to touch. She kept waiting for aggression that just didn't happen. All he seemed to want were kisses, the exploring of her lips, the cherishing of them.

It had been years...years...since she'd tasted a kiss that promised and wooed. She felt her hands clench into loose fists at her sides, her heart beat and then skip a beat. Warmth. Such a simple thing. The feeling of two people against a very cold world, a sharing of the texture of loneliness, the flavor of a sweet ache...the flavor of his mouth.

Her lips suddenly trembled violently under his. She couldn't remember how to breathe. At sixteen this was exactly what she'd missed...exactly what she'd never found since. She felt wooed back to the time when she was innocent, to the time before the whole damn world had gone wrong, to the time when a kiss was everything. And she couldn't stop trembling.

Sam raised his head, and stared with brooding stillness down into her eyes. "Leslie," he said softly.

His voice broke the magic, collided with reality. She wasn't innocent. She wasn't sixteen. And she had no business shaking like a virgin—not with her past.

She groped for the doorknob but his fingers curled around her wrist before she could escape. At that contact, she stiffened. His other hand curled under her chin, raising it. "No," he said gently, correctly reading the anxiety in her eyes. His tone turned thoughtful. "I'm not going to keep you—or press. But I want you to know that you sure don't kiss like a lady who's taken on this man's army, honey. In fact, a man might almost believe..."

She could have rehearsed the short, sultry laugh. "Pierce, I've kissed more men in my life than most women even meet in a lifetime. You wanted a kiss, you got one. I owed you that for the sunburn I caused you, and believe me, it's nothing to me."

He let her go after that, rather fast. Exactly what she wanted.

Four

When a woman doesn't sleep half the night, she naturally wakes up a little touchy. The first thing Leslie said to Sam the next morning was a crisp "I heard you turn on the computer last night around midnight. You do it again, and I leave on the next plane out, Pierce. Got it?"

"Loud and clear." His tone could have melted butter.

"Stay completely away from that computer screen."

"Fine."

"In fact, stay completely away from your work and all printed material of any kind."

"You're the boss," Sam said amiably. "Anything else?"

She drilled him all morning, and by one p.m. there was a fine mist of rain outside. Sam gave her one fleeting look when she announced they were going for a run, but for two hours he jogged behind her in the cold downpour. They returned home sopping wet and chilled and she knew darn well she'd given his unused muscles a workout. He never said a word.

The next day she set up a new exercise for him. Harry found her the two-by-four; she found the rocks to balance under it. She had Sam walk the plank, forward, then backward, then on one foot, then the other. There was no better exercise for teaching linear focus and balance; Leslie could have told him that but didn't. She waited for him to complain, to say one word—she knew the exercises mortified him, that it was killing him to do them in front of a woman—but he said nothing.

The fourth afternoon she took him on a hike that would have exhausted a marine recruit. Still nothing. No matter what she told him to do, he simply gave her that genial smile and did it.

The man had clearly been put on earth to drive her personally nuts. She gave him far more reasons than any sane man would require to mutiny. Dammit, if he raised his voice once she could justify going home. Sam obviously wasn't sane. He was a perfect lamb. He never mentioned kisses, he never mentioned private lives and he never challenged anything she did or said. She couldn't wear an outfit provocative enough to make him look below her neck.

On their fifth afternoon together, she was pacing in front of the cabin door, glancing at her watch every thirty seconds or so. It was fifteen after one. Ten minutes ago, Sam had been ordered upstairs to come up with a bathing suit before they headed out. She knew darn well she'd sounded like a shrew.

He'd answered, "Of course, Leslie," in that peculiarly gentle voice he'd started using lately—the one that made her think of a man soothing a wounded fawn.

Of course, Leslie. Of course, Leslie. The refrain sounded in her temples like a hammer of a headache. How dare he be so blasted nice when she'd acted like the Wicked Witch of the West toward him?

She glanced at her watch again, then turned tormented eyes to the cabin when the screen door finally banged open. Sam loped down the steps with two towels over his shoulder and wearing nothing more than jeans and sneakers. His shoulders and chest were a fine golden bronze; after only a few days of exercise his muscles had toned up. His flesh wrapped around sinew in smooth brown ripples whenever he moved. Her flesh burned, looking at him.

There was a small problem in taking on the transformation of a man: one got results. Sam had been reasonably good-looking when she met him. He was slowly but surely turning into a downright lady-killer, and never mind his peeling nose. Those fathomless gray eyes leveled on her, and she could feel her pulse tick like a time bomb. All he had to do was look at her and she felt as soft as butter. It had to stop, once and for all.

"Ready to go?" she demanded sharply.

"Whenever you are."

"Not even going to ask me where we're going today, Sam?"

"Wherever you want," he said mildly.

"I had a feeling you'd say that," she muttered and started off.

The day was hot. Sultry air whispered through the pines and made the air heavy with the scents of earth and trees. She barely noticed, taking the shortest route down the ravine and up again. She pushed past tree branches and brush. They'd run across a stream on one of their hikes. All she intended to do was get there by the shortest route possible.

There was a rock climb, then a long slope of green, then thick, tangled woods. Her red shorts were sticking to her skin by the time she reached the shade of woods. The black halter top molded to her breasts like glue. There were shorts and halter tops...and then there were shorts and halter tops. The ones she was wearing were of the more provocative variety, because she'd been in the mood. "Dress for success" was a hackneyed concept but it was one Leslie believed in. She just interpreted it differently than most.

She heard the dance and trickle of water before they reached it, and her step quickened. Minutes later, she pushed through the last of low undergrowth that nearly obscured the stream. The flow of water started high, dawdled between trees perched at impossible angles on the mountain, then rushed down in the splash of a small waterfall to form a sweet, clear, cold pool. The wonder of it, the delight of it, was that the water kept on moving from there and seemed to actually fall off the earth. The cliff was a sheer drop and the view was of searing blue sky.

"We stop here," she told Sam, and perched on a long flat rock where she could tug off her sneakers. Heat never bothered her, she loved it, yet she couldn't wait another moment before immersing her toes in the clear water. One toe was nearly enough, however. The pool was ice-cold.

Sam dropped down beside her, and she stiffened. "The lesson for this afternoon is right in front of you," she informed him. "Focusing is completely different underwater."

Leaning down from the rock, he let his hand trail in the water. "That's not water. That's an iceberg in disguise," he mentioned wryly.

"You're tough," she assured him, heard the taunt in her own voice and felt despair. She was getting exceedingly tired of being a shrew.

"You're the boss." He stood up beside her, so that his long tall shadow blocked the sun.

At first, she didn't specifically pay any attention as he disrobed—not when his canvas shoes landed beside her, nor when his jeans were tossed at her feet. It was the jockey shorts that startled her—first because they were navy blue and not conventional white—and then because it was obvious Sam hadn't been wearing swimming trunks under his jeans. For that matter, when a man removes jockey shorts, it's pretty darn doubtful he's wearing anything else.

She heard the splash when he hit the water, then heard a man's yelp that couldn't help but make her chuckle. A moment later he surfaced, his wet head glistening in the sun. "It's damn cold," he announced. "Focusing, of course, is terrific."

"Wonderful," she said weakly. The ripples from the splash were fading fast. The pool couldn't be more clear just below her. He was only standing waist-deep and she could see the exact line where his tan turned white and a water-magnified... abruptly she froze, her arms wrapped around her knees and her fanny totally uncomfortable on hard rock.

He made a shallow dive—she closed her eyes too late to miss the view of one muscular white hip. And then for a time he was underwater, coming up only intermittently for a burst of air.

Five minutes became fifteen, then twenty. Anxiety started to gnaw at her. The pool was too cold to stay in for long; he'd get a cramp. Twenty minutes turned into a half an hour, and a frown slowly burned "guilty" into her forehead, even if no one else could see it.

The instant he surfaced the next time, she called out, "Will you get out of there?"

"I thought the lesson this afternoon was—"

"Get *out*, Pierce." He'd walked from chest-high water to waist-high water before she jerked to her feet. "Wait a minute; I'll throw you the towel."

"Thanks." He caught it midair and had to clamp his teeth together to keep his jaws from chattering. His lips were blue and his skin felt like a wet suit freshly dipped in the Arctic. He used the towel to dry his hair.

She'd had in mind he use the towel to wrap around him where it mattered. Cheeks flushed, she averted her eyes when he climbed onto the rock. He spread the towel next to her, and flopped down on his stomach. When she looked sideways, all she could see was his wet head and the tips of his shoulders, but water was shimmering between goose bumps, and the color of his skin was ruddy blue. Shame racked her. She'd done it again. Pushed him, knowing the man would never turn down the dare. Sam was one of those men who had to be strong, she'd known it from the beginning.

He murmured, "Is it going to be against the rules if I warm up for a few minutes in the sun?"

"Of course not."

"I didn't know," he said mildly. "I figured we'd be off on another twenty-mile hike the minute we finished that . . . focusing exercise."

Leslie studied the nails on her left hand, and for the first time since she was ten years old, bit one. It was important that he not like her. She'd certainly done everything but stand on her head to make sure he didn't.

The problem was that she increasingly cared for him—and that included getting his opinion, his respect. He was so damned . . . human. Foolishly sensitive about his inability to read, foolishly sensitive about being a brain. He was ridiculously hard on himself, and it hadn't taken her long to discover he was a good man, a man of integrity and standards. Not a man for her—definitely not a man for her.

The right woman could give him confidence and make absolutely positive he enjoyed a little life instead of burying himself in work. Sam so badly needed a woman—but the right kind of woman. Not her. Her heart kept trying to trip her up, convince her the empathy that flowed between them when they were working was real. It wasn't real. Maybe Sam had suffered from labels just as she had, but their nature was completely different. Sam had been burdened with the label "brain" and then had hoisted one on himself for failing to read. One could rise above those kinds of labels.

Once upon a time, she'd been a sixteen-year-old virgin who'd suffered the label "slut" in a small town.

Her eyes closed against the bright sunlight, remembering. Being around Sam always seemed to force her to remember. At sixteen, she'd nearly died from the injustice of it. She'd been too damn young to know how to fight back. But even so, the mistake she had made was not a forgivable one. Not a mistake one could forget or forgive. And she knew exactly what Sam would think of her if he knew. It was far better if he simply thought she was a bitch.

But if the man lying next to her didn't put on some clothes darn soon, she was going to have a heart attack. Without turning her head, she stole another glance at him out of the corner of her eye. His shoulders were dry, baking in the sun. The goose bumps were gone. His eyes were closed, thick lashes casting shadows on his cheekbones.

"You should have told me you didn't have a suit," she said irritably.

"Did it matter? You made it pretty clear that you'd seen your share of naked men before. I couldn't imagine that you'd care—"

"Of course I don't," she snapped, and glared at the fingernail she'd just chewed off. Wasn't that enough protection? That he thought she'd slept with a cast of thousands? "Pierce?"

"Hmm?"

She tried to make her voice matter-of-fact and cold, but both guilt and an apology were trying to bubble over in her need to explain. "Look—I can't help it if the plank and the circles are awkward for you to do. I'm used to teaching younger kids, teenagers. They think the exercises are fun; that's partly how I discovered them. And they're the best exercises I know for teaching focusing and balance. That's the truth."

He said nothing, annoying her.

"And about your not working on the computer, or reading. Darnit, that's important. It's an issue of bad habits, Pierce. If I were explaining it to a ten-year-old, I'd be saying that your eyes are unhappy with you. When you force them to see an entire page as a whole, you're asking those eyes to do triple the work that a normal person's eyes have to do. Eyes *want* to focus linearly. And once they're retrained, they will, and often enough that process can be darned fast because your eyes want to do it the right way. But not if you mess them up by exposing them to old habits in the meantime."

He didn't so much as open his eyes, but after a time he murmured lazily, "I guessed all that."

He'd also guessed that if he gave her enough rope, she'd hang herself. And she'd done it again. She'd tried very hard to be a perfect witch, until guilt worked her up into a fine anxiety attack. The first anxiety attack had brought her to his bedroom after dark. This one had her chewing her nails.

"You *guessed* that?"

"I figured all along you knew what you were doing. Or were doing what you felt you had to do. Leslie?"

"What?"

"Granted that you've been very clear on what terms you're willing to stay here. But could we drop the rules for one short minute? I mean that literally. No more than sixty seconds."

She gave him a wary "Yes," which was followed by Sam's richly vibrant, "Good." Immediately she was assaulted by the startling sensation of Sam scooping her up in long strong arms. He was on his feet before she'd caught her breath; climbing down from the rock before she'd started the first sputtering protest. And she could hear the splash of water around his feet long before she'd guessed what he'd intended.

When his arms released her, there was a short moment when she was suspended in air. Then water enveloped her, enclosing her sunbaked body in icy silk. She came up gasping, both tingling and numb from the shock of the cold pool, her hair streaming down her face in wet rivulets. For that instant, she was so furious she was speechless, and couldn't stop shivering long enough to push her hair back so she could see. By the time she jammed her hair back she discovered she was glaring in the wrong direction, and when she finally whirled around, Sam had already climbed on the rock again and was calmly knotting the towel around his hips and dropping to a stomach-down position.

Gray eyes met hers over the distance of sun and clear blue water. His grin was all boy. "That felt good," he said feelingly.

"You..." Rage petered out for no real reason. He had such a beautiful grin. A matching smile helplessly curved her lips that somehow turned into a burst of laughter. "Darnit, I deserved that, didn't I?"

"You certainly did." No question of his sincerity.

Surging to waist-deep water, her hands perched on her hips. "It's cold!"

"No kidding?"

"My hair—my clothes—"

"Pity," he said without a trace of it in his voice. "Your clothes will dry in ten minutes if you lay them on the rock in the sun. Just wrap yourself up in a towel."

"You brought two," she noticed belatedly as she carefully traveled the stones at the pool's edge in her bare feet. That fast, the hot sun was soothing away the shivers—except where her halter and shorts clung like sticky ice.

As she climbed the rocks, Sam turned on his side, judging her like a two-year-old that had created a monster...and was delighted with it. Her makeup was gone; her hair was dripping in bedraggled Shirley Temple fashion and he wasn't opposed to the display of nipples and breasts that her wet halter top offered him. More than that, he'd heard her laughter and discovered that Leslie could direct it at herself.

"You planned this," she said accusingly, but her red lips were still curved in a wide grin.

"Nonsense. How could I have? I didn't know what you had in store for the afternoon." He handed her a towel. "It's been a long time since I seriously planned a teacher's demise—for heaven's sake, get out of those clothes before you freeze to death—her name was Mrs. Riverby. I was eight. I used to dream about the woman. About putting glue on her chair, attacking her fat rear end with spitballs, putting tarantulas on her desk—"

"What a monster of a kid you must have been." For an instant she just stood there on the rock. Sam had turned his head, closed his eyes. Rationally, she knew her clothes would dry faster if she removed them. Rationally, she knew she'd given Sam every reason to believe she was comfortable with nudity and men, and he certainly hadn't thought a thing about lying there in front of her without a stitch on.

"I wasn't a monster of a kid," Sam said from behind closed eyes. "I was an angel. A paragon. Teacher's pet. Those were all just dreams. I had real courage on a level with a wrinkled carrot. But someone should have used those spitballs on that woman."

She laughed, and reached back for the strings of

her halter top. Either the fabric was wet or her fingers were having a sit-down strike, because she couldn't make the strings untie. Finally she wrapped a towel around herself and with miraculous ease undid her wet clothes from the inside. The procedure was awkward, long and silly. Sam hadn't once opened his eyes. "Sounds to me," she said lightly, "like you never had much of a chance to just be a normal, mischievous kid."

"Eggheads are supposed to be born serious."

With her shorts and top arranged in the sun, she tied the towel tighter around her breasts and dropped down next to him on her back. "Were you? Overserious as a kid?"

"Yup. Deadly dull. I spent all day in school on mathematics and came home from school to do more mathematics, and all I wanted in life was to play basketball."

"Basketball!" Her laughter turned soft, her smile protective. "Dammit, Sam, didn't they even let you do that? What kind of parents did you have, anyway?"

"Caring parents, loving parents. They were just normal people who were terrified out of their minds because they didn't have a normal kid. All they wanted was to do the right thing by me. Philosophies have changed since then—these days there's the concept of a well-rounded emotional environment. But when I was growing up, a kid with a few smarts was deliberately isolated from the mainstream. That wasn't my parents' fault.''

"Tell me about the schools you went to."

He told her about the feelings he'd had as a child. He told her things he'd never told a soul—but when had he ever discussed feelings with anyone? It was the first natural conversation he'd had with her, and there was no way on earth he was going to stop it. It was as if dunking her in the pool had broken the ice, made her forget the masks she wore.

As he talked he watched her hair curl as it dried in the sun. He watched her closed eyes—the way the damp, thick lashes shuttered on her cheeks; he watched a droplet of water hovering like a diamond between her breasts just at the break of the towel. He watched her stretch like a kitten in the sun when she was finally warm again.

He wished to hell he had more experience with women. Four nights before, a simple kiss had thrown him into an abyss. He'd expected a practiced skill, something to match her sultry looks. Instead she'd kissed like a maiden, a lass who didn't know whose lips went where. He'd never imagined dynamite packaged in violets, dew in spring, an untouched rose in the morning.

How was he supposed to sleep after that?

So he hadn't. He'd plotted. Those few kisses might have been illusion; he had to know. And right now, with the sun beating down on both of them, seemed the best of times to find out.

"Sam?" Leslie's eyes blinked open, aware suddenly that he hadn't answered her last question. She'd never heard him move, never guessed that he was suddenly close. The shadow of his head blocked the sun. All she could see was silver-gray eyes, deeper than the turn of a diamond, and a man's mouth slowly dropping to hers. Her heart hammered danger in her chest and her brain scrambled for defenses.

Then his lips touched hers, claiming them. His mouth was warm, smooth, gentle. It frightened her that she suddenly couldn't hear the flow of water, the birds, the rustle of a fretful breeze in the far woods. Those things were real. Feeling like a fragile buttercup was not real. Feeling lazy and fluid and helpless . . . the kiss was a tender hello, nothing more. A little kiss shouldn't change the world.

The sun-baked rock was gritty beneath her back, the soles of her feet, her palms. She didn't move, refused to breathe. Sam's lips moved over hers, nibbling at the bottom one, tasting the top. His tongue slid out to trace the closed line; she didn't open her mouth. He shifted, his arm beneath her neck forcing her head back, and his free hand smoothed into her hair before his lips came down again.

She'd never parted her lips—she was sure of it— yet their tongues suddenly met and mated. She felt his fingers in her hair, his thumb gently brushing her cheek. A coiled ache rolled through her, escaped in the sound of a low, sweet whimper. He mustn't. He mustn't. He kissed with such hunger, and the sun kept beating down. It was too hot, and she didn't know what to do with the softness threatening to melt her.

His lips left hers to roam her cheeks, her closed eyelids, her temples. Where he touched, she felt brand-new. His palm strayed down to the beat of pulse in her throat, and he wooed that pulse with the stroke of his thumb. The caress was delicate, as if he believed her fragile, precious. Worse than that, she felt fragile, precious.

Reality returned, but not as it was before. The sound of moving water roared in her ears. The scent of warmth and man entered her lungs. She tasted sunlight, and then Sam again. She tasted a sweet summer breeze, and then Sam again. Her heart wouldn't beat right, and everything around her seemed to be trembling but her.

His lips were on her throat when she felt his fingers at the knot of her towel. His palm caressed her shoulder, her bare collarbone. She reached for him unconsciously, contacted bare, warm, hair-covered chest; her hand jerked back.

His palm closed on her hand; he pushed it back in place, spreading her fingers on his chest like a man showing an untried woman what to do—what he wanted, what he needed. The flat of her palm rested on the hard button of his nipple; the thump of his heart astounded her.

And his hand was back, kneading her shoulder, whispering over her collarbone, roaming to the first swell of her breast as lips touched lips again. The kiss was shy, disarming her. His mouth touched and withdrew, touched and withdrew. His palm gently moved lower, taking in more than the first swell of breast. The heart of his hand cradled her nipple. Heat flooded her and she knew too suddenly that she was the one who was trembling.

"I can't," she whispered. "Sam—don't."

He didn't move his hand, but his lips brushed her cheek again, into her hair, soothing her, quieting her. "Why?"

"Because—" she groped "—I told you. I have . . . relationships at home."

"Your two men."

"Actually, there are three."

Dark eyes glinted down at her with sudden fierceness and anger. Yet his breath hovered over her lips and his tone was gentle. "Ah, three men now, is it?"

"I . . . yes. Three."

His lips nibbled again. "Your love life is a hell of a lot more complicated than mine, sunshine. I haven't had a woman in months. And I wouldn't begin to know how to juggle two at a time, much less three."

"Sam—"

"I won't complicate things for you, but I'm afraid I'm going to have to hold you for one good long minute before I let you go."

"No. Sam. Listen to me—"

"Yes."

He slid a long leg between hers and slowly wrapped his arms around her, using his body to cushion her against the hard rock. He leveled his mouth on hers because she would have talked if he hadn't. In his head he mentally started counting off the sixty seconds, because he meant what he said. After a minute he was letting her go, because if he didn't do it then, he knew damn well he wasn't going to, ever.

Too much of this didn't make sense. True, the feel of her length-to-length against him made perfect sense. Her sweet breath, her perfect breasts cradled to his chest, his arousal pressed against her stomach, his leg clamped between hers, the intimacy—all of that made perfect sense. The scent of her alone was magic. Her silky skin belonged to him, her mouth for that moment was his, her pelvis cradled against him: nothing in his entire life had ever made as much sense.

Her reactions were what confused him. Her mouth told him she was willing, so did the hard, hot nubbins of her nipples. But once he'd managed to push aside the towels, the shudder that passed through her body at that first intimate contact was the tremble of a woman unsure and awkward. He caught the faintest glimpse of dark-brown eyes, chocolate soft, glazed, desperate. Frightened? At the initial feel of his arousal, her legs had contracted around him, then shuddered back; a shy glow colored her face and breasts as if her own first reaction had startled her. And her hands . . . her hands hovered in midair, half clenched, as if they were separate from her body and lost, not knowing at all what to do with themselves.

Sixty seconds passed all too fast. He lifted his mouth, let his brooding eyes settle on hers for several more moments, and murmured softly, "Around my neck, honey. That's where you put your arms. It's so simple." Then he unwrapped himself from her in one long harsh breath and forced himself to stand and reach for his clothes.

For an instant Leslie couldn't move. The pool, the shadowed woods in the distance, the sun in her hair—all of it disoriented her. Then she groped for the towel and her clothes, turning away from him while her fingers fumbled with the zipper of her shorts that wouldn't zip, the straps of her halter that refused to tie.

His hands suddenly brushed hers aside at the nape of her neck. He tied the tie. "Listen," she said hesitantly.

He was silent, listening.

She couldn't imagine what she was going to say. There wasn't a coherent thought in her head. She felt panic and wonder and this lazy heat that didn't want to leave her body. There was anger that the lamb had always really been the lion in wait; there was desire. She had a horrible premonition that there was no going back to the obedient-student/bitchy-teacher relationship she'd set up. Leslie was feeling tricked but not feeling tricked at all at the same time. After all, he hadn't pushed, he hadn't pressed; he'd been so incredibly gentle and giving in touch. She was miserably confused.

"Ready to start back home?"

She nodded, her face down as she tied her canvas shoes. When she stood up again, he dropped a lazy arm around her shoulder and they started for the woods. Bright sun became soothing dark shade, but her heart kept beating, pounding in her chest.

"Les?" he said casually.

"Hmm?"

"While we're walking home, you want to tell me a little about all your...men? Not to pry. But your private life's been so disrupted by these three weeks because of me, and if you want to unload a little of that..." His tone was friendly, warm, carefully un-threatening.

"Yes." A sigh of relief rushed from her lips. Establishing a barrier again was exactly what she needed to do. The invention of other men had always effectively created that barrier for her.

Sam heard about Gordon, Jake and Logan. She threw in a Steven when there was a short burst of silence. Her bedroom had a revolving door, she'd have him believe. One man was barely out before another was scheduled in.

He'd never heard such poppycock in his entire life, but by the time they reached home she was relaxed again. His little liar entered the house ahead of him with a sway of feminine hips that nearly sent him over the edge. Then he had a better thought of exactly what Leslie would be like if she truly were sent over the edge.

It was a thought he couldn't get out of his head.

Five

It stormed the next morning. By noon a weak sun was peeking out from behind clouds and a lazy mist flowed in and around the mountain peaks. Leslie stared out the kitchen window at all the freshly washed leaves, all the greens bursting to life. Yellow cinquefoils and white clumps of wild buckwheat seemed to spring up inches at a time from the drenching rain. Huge pink elephant's-head blossoms thrived, even under the shade trees.

She turned quickly when she heard the thud of Harry's heavy footstep in the doorway. "Now, I don't know what you're wanting for lunch but I'll be making it today," he told her.

"I'll help."

"No, no. You just rest and relax."

They had the same argument every day. Whoever had designed the oak and French-blue kitchen had country charm in mind, but hadn't planned for space. Two people couldn't move between refrigerator and sink without bumping into each other, though Harry tiptoed around her whenever possible. He gave her a guilty look after opening a can of ravioli for himself and setting it to simmer on the stove. Then he gradually eased closer until he was looking over her shoulder.

"What're you making for you two?"

"A shrimp salad—shrimp, fresh peas, celery, lettuce and a very special dressing." She smiled at him over her shoulder. "There's more than enough for you, too. Harry, you can't just eat starch *every* meal."

"Well, I might try a little."

Leslie already knew that he would. She'd never convert either man to yogurt, but they both acted as if they'd never seen fresh food before. She was just claiming the herbal tea from the back porch when Sam walked in.

Wearing denims and a burgundy cotton pullover that buttoned at the throat, he looked much more like a lumberjack than a man who spent his life at a desk. His eyes whisked over her white jeans, her open-weave black sweater, the black headband intended to hold her curls at bay although her hair never behaved in humid weather. He smiled.

She felt silly rainbows curling up in her stomach. This was a crazy feeling, being friends with him. He...liked her. It had never occurred to her that a man could simply *like* her. After yesterday afternoon at the pool, she'd been so tense...but not afterward, and not this morning.

The stories she'd told him about the other men in her life were darn near enough to make her cheeks burn. The thing was, he'd kept asking, then she'd kept embellishing, and the whole thing had become rather complicated. She didn't know what had happened to her at that mountain pool, but it certainly couldn't be allowed to happen again. Sam was a conservative man, a private, possessive man. Every feminine instinct promised her that he'd never pursue an intimate relationship with a woman who had bedded half the boys in Minnesota. He'd want a woman who was, well, *his*.

She knew this because he'd said so. After dinner last night, they'd dragged chairs outside and sat in the moonlight, blankets wrapped around themselves when the night grew chill. There'd been no touch, no kiss, no invitation—just talk. He'd asked her more about her men, her life. She'd kept waiting for a feeling of being judged that just didn't happen. He'd made it more than clear that he was fascinated by their different life-styles. What was the harm in two people sharing experiences who would never meet again?

Well, there was harm, and Leslie knew that. But Sam had confessed what he'd found valuable to him in his relationships with women—loyalty, trust, faithfulness—things she'd led him to believe were unimportant to her. He wouldn't touch her. Honor— the old-fashioned value—reeked from Sam. There were very few honorable men in this life.

And there were very few men who'd made her simply laugh and talk. Who'd ever just accepted her. She'd slept with that feeling of warmth, and this morning they'd worked with a new easiness between them. Now, as she set the salad in front of him, he gave her a wink, and she felt the silliest urge to laugh for no reason at all. "What?" she started to question, but he motioned her to silence as Harry dropped into the chair across from him.

"Going trout fishing this afternoon, Harry?"

"Sure enough." Harry had both dishes in front of him—the canned ravioli and the salad—just in case the latter proved unpalatable. "Biggest trout I've ever seen in that Jackson Lake." He watched Leslie unfold a napkin and hastily reached for his. "What are you two up to this afternoon?"

"We're going into town," Sam said smoothly.

Leslie glanced up. Harry's fork poised midair. "You can't go into town. You know that," Harry said.

"Afraid we have to."

"No way. You need something, I'll get it for you."

"It's not my choice," Sam said regretfully. "It's for Leslie."

Both Leslie's brows raised in surprise. Sam's foot gently clamped on hers under the table.

"Oh." Harry took a breath, his harsh tone automatically softening when he looked at her across the table. "I'll get you absolutely anything you need, sweetheart. You just make me out a list. The thing is, though, Pierce here's had too many pictures in the national papers since he won that award thing. We can't have him out in public; we don't want either of you out in the public. We want you both here, where you're nice and safe."

"It's not my choice," Sam repeated regretfully. "She says I have to. For one thing, she says I need to practice focusing while driving."

Leslie gave up trying to eat and cupped her chin in her palm.

"All right. So the three of us can drive a few backcountry roads this afternoon," Harry said firmly.

"But it isn't just driving. She needs some supplies from town. Supplies she has to have if I'm going to read."

"Oh." Harry abruptly shoved back his fluff of hair. "Well, that's the thing we're all here for; I don't want to interfere with any of that, but nothing I can get for you myself?" he said unhappily.

Sam never looked at her, but under the table she could feel the firm pressure of his ankle against hers.

Leslie said, "Ah... no, unfortunately." She added absently, "Actually, I do need a mirror."

"A mirror? There's mirrors in both bathrooms."

"Not that kind of mirror. I need a mirror of a size that I can move around—there's an exercise that has to do with Sam's dyslexia."

"And it isn't just that," Sam intervened, showing not the least surprise at her invention of a mirror. "She's got a page-long shopping list of stuff she says she has to have—only I also have to be there, to make sure it all works."

"You mean, like, it has to be sort of fitted to him?"

Leslie hesitated.

"Exactly, Harry," Sam agreed.

Harry rubbed the part of his stomach where his ulcer was kicking in and looked helplessly at Leslie.

"You know," she said gently, "I do have several years of self-defense behind me, Harry. It's not as if he would be... unprotected." She frowned, critically studying Sam. "Don't you think we could fix him up—put dark glasses on him, part his hair in the middle, stuff like that—so that all those spies running around Jackson Hole wouldn't recognize him?"

Harry's fingers pressed on the knot of acid in his abdomen. "Now, neither of you take this seriously, I know. But there are a lot of nuts in this world, and it's my job to make sure you're both safe. I've got my orders, Pierce, you know that."

Sam's eyes sent her a sharp silver message across the table. The only thing was, she couldn't read it. She didn't understand any of this...except that Sam obviously wanted to get out for the afternoon. And he was counting on her for an alibi and the assistance to get past their watchdog. The tiny conspiracy very definitely struck her sense of humor; more than that, she felt the silkiest fluid feeling at the thought of Sam needing her.

She paused, and then leaned over the table. Her soft lashes fluttered on her cheeks, then raised slowly to Harry. Her palm covered the older man's rough one. "Please, Harry?" she said softly.

"Oh, God." His cheeks turned bright pink and his ulcer was going to kill him for sure. "Oh, God."

Sam had a sudden fit of coughing and rose from the table.

"I hope you feel good and guilty," Leslie muttered as she climbed into the Jeep.

Sam started the engine. "*Me?* If I'd batted my eyes at Harry like that, he'd have fed me a tonic of straight whiskey and called in the National Guard."

"You know he's going to worry—"

"Harry loves to worry. And you and I deserve an afternoon off."

"Is that what all that was about?" she demanded.

"No, actually." Behind his dark glasses, she couldn't see his eyes. "I really did want some things from town. I had an idea... Never mind. We'll leave that as a surprise."

"What surprise?"

He shook his head.

"I can't stand surprises," she announced.

But she could certainly hand them out, he thought fleetingly. It was like working with a puzzle, trying to fathom what was real and what wasn't. The seductive trick she'd pulled on Harry was one of her games. Those "years of self-defense" she'd mentioned—he had an idea that was true. If he waited for Leslie to come through with a little solid honesty, he figured he'd have to wait until the next century.

So if he cared, it was up to him to fathom the real lady. He cared. She never seemed to bother with small lies, just the big ones. She was a skilled fibber, but one who could be tripped up with a little effort. Her Gordon, for instance, couldn't have both brown and blue eyes. And her Steven and her Logan couldn't both occupy her Wednesday nights, unless she liked a crowded bed.

She touched like a woman who'd been locked in a convent, not like one who indulged in regular orgies. And sometime while she was talking the night before, his heart had kicked in an announcement— no one lied like that unless they had something to hide. The lady was running scared. Of what he had no idea, and he knew damn well he didn't have the experience with women to ever completely trust that intuition. Judging by her outside, any man could see she needed no one to look after her. However, his heart kept telling him that she not only needed a man's protection, but also that she was lonely and frightened and vulnerable.

And that she could care for him?

You're already in way over your head. Let's not be too much of a fool, Pierce, his heart advised him. "Look," he murmured to Leslie.

She had to twist her head around to see the huge moose lapping from the narrow creek below them. The creature made her laugh—he was massive but so misproportioned. His legs were spindly and his head almost as big as his body. Then the road turned again, and a herd of pronghorn scattered in a green valley between cliffs in the distance. Closer to town, she saw a pair of elk rambling along the road next to them. Everywhere and always, the craggy winter-topped mountains backdropped by a blue sky that just kept coming.

"God's country," Sam murmured.

She flashed him a smile. "Yes." She knew the wild country of upper Minnesota, but it was nothing like this. She'd known Jackson Hole was a ski resort in the winter, but she hadn't expected the charm of the Western town. The streets were flooded with ten-gallon hats and men with big turquoise-studded belt buckles and cowboy boots. Sam kept driving in circles until she finally looked at him.

"Are we ever going to park?" she asked casually.

"Just getting my bearings. First, do you or don't you need that mirror thing?"

"I need it—if there's someplace we can find one." She cocked her head. "I told you at lunch—"

"I know," he said wryly. There was just no telling what was fib or what was made up with Les. "All right. I've got two priorities here—the main one is an ice-cream cone."

"Ice-cream cone?"

"Double dip. Chocolate mint—but that'll wait." He motioned through the front window of the Jeep. "There's a hardware store where you should be able to get some kind of mirror. How about meeting back here in about twenty minutes?"

"I...fine." She was still chuckling at the grown man's craving for an ice-cream cone when she walked back out of the hardware store five minutes later. She popped the mirror in the back seat of the Jeep and glanced around. Sam was nowhere.

Pulling her purse onto her shoulder, she pushed her hands in her pockets and wandered a little distance, absorbing the sounds and sights of Jackson Hole while she waited for him. She paused in front of a shop window that carried Western-style shirts with rhinestone trim, and grinned. Sam would die before wearing one of them. But the cream five-gallon hat...she could picture that on his tawny head. When he was relaxed, he had a loose, rangy stride that made her think of rugged men and just this sort of country.

She paused in front of the next shop window. There was only one thing in it. A woman's blouse— pale pink, with a scooped cameolike lace inset and long sleeves, in a fabric that looked crushably soft. She took a step away from it and then came back, her eyes turning wistful. It was ridiculous to want the thing. She'd worn bold colors for years—not pastels. Only a sweet kind of woman could choose a blouse like that. A soft woman. A lady.

"It'd look terrific on you," Sam said from behind her.

She whirled around, and immediately noticed his empty hands. "You didn't get what you wanted?"

He nodded. "I already stored it in the Jeep—more than enough to convince Harry we needed this trip," he said wryly and motioned to the blouse again. "You want to go in and see if they have it in your size?"

She shook her head and took a step away from the window. "Of course not."

"Why?"

Like a tall, stubborn mule, he appeared to be parked in front of the silly pink blouse. She sighed. "Pierce, all you have to do is look at me to know that powder pink isn't my style."

He looked at the blouse, then back at her again, and frowned. "What are you talking about? I think it looks exactly your style."

Sun suddenly glistened in her eyes. She wished it were, that was all. When she was with Sam, she wanted to wear pastels and spray on perfume with the scent of daffodils and...just be young again. Good again. Sam deserved a lady.

But Leslie couldn't take back time.

"Hey. Where's the fire?" Sam caught up with her and launched an arm around her shoulders to slow her down. Her features had gone pale; her eyes looked huge and never mind the defiant tilt to her chin.

"I was headed for your ice-cream cone," she said swiftly. "I'm fairly sure I saw a sign near the corner—"

"Leslie—"

"Chocolate mint for you, tasteless creature that you are. But they'd better darn well have butter pecan."

He hesitated, but already knew it would be a mistake to press her. He tried a smile, hoping to put her at ease again. "Or else?"

"I've torn up bigger towns than this when a serious craving for butter pecan hit, Pierce. So be warned."

Sam dropped thirty years when he had an ice-cream cone in his hand, she discovered. His tongue flicked over the smooth confection and he closed his eyes as if he'd just discovered sin. They walked the streets of Jackson Hole, nibbling their cones, and the only reason she didn't move away from his arm around her shoulders was because she couldn't. A man crossing streets with his eyes closed was a traffic menace. Once the first angry car honked at them, she wrapped her arm around his waist and did some serious steering.

"I haven't had an ice-cream cone in years," he confessed.

"No kidding?"

"No one with any sense would choose butter pecan when chocolate mint is available."

"And I thought you were supposed to be so intelligent," she said with despair, but then her tone turned thoughtful. "Don't you think we should get a little something for Harry before we go back?"

"For Harry? Why?" He stopped, licked his forefinger and then reached down to dab at the corner of her mouth as if she'd missed a drop of butter pecan. She hadn't, but it was certainly a darn good excuse to touch her. An arm around her shoulder wasn't enough.

"Because Harry deserves a gift—he'll have been worried." Sam was looking at her so intently that she worried she had an ice-cream moustache. She licked her lips. Nothing came away sticky, but Sam abruptly looked like a man in pain.

Sam took a long breath and tried to remember the thread of conversation. "We have to get Harry a present because he'll have worried?"

After five stores, she finally settled on a box of chocolate-covered cherries. Sam would have preferred a ten-mile hike in the hills to shopping, but just as they were walking back to the Jeep, he asked casually, "Need any souvenirs for your people back home?"

"Souvenirs? Who on earth would I buy..." She hesitated, then said smoothly, "Oh, you mean like for Doug?"

Doug? A new name to add to her male harem. "Yeah, like him," Sam agreed.

"I probably should," she said thoughtfully, her eyes carefully peeled on the traffic ahead, "but we're already late. Maybe another time."

Rather than strangle her, he slammed the door just a little too forcefully once she was in the Jeep. The lady was considerate enough to worry about getting a present for a gruff old codger who couldn't mean beans to her, but not interested in presents for the endless number of men she claimed to be passionately, intimately, exhilaratingly in love with.

Sure.

Harry raved over the chocolates but was totally dumbfounded at the air mattresses and sleeping bags that emerged from their hiding place under a tarp in the back of the Jeep.

"It's for night vision," Sam repeated.

"But what does that have to do with—"

Sam said patiently, "When you strengthen night focusing power, you strengthen the eye's natural ability to perform under unnatural light conditions. Just ask her, Harry."

Harry turned perplexed eyes to Leslie.

Leslie had never heard such nonsense in her entire life. "Sam..."

Harry shook his head. "Never mind, never mind. I don't even want to hear. I'm going in to make dinner. You two just keep on ... doing whatever you're doing."

As soon as Harry was in the house, Leslie took another look at Sam's purchases, propped her hands on her hips, and said wryly, "All right. I give. What is it *you* think we're doing?"

"You mean the sleeping bags? Isn't it obvious?"

"Nope." All afternoon, her defenses had been gradually slipping. Sam had been friendly, easy and naturally affectionate. A man seeking a lover didn't regularly and casually bring up a woman's ongoing affairs. She wanted to believe that she was building something with Sam she'd never had with another man: just a friendship. "Just a friendship" was precious stuff to Leslie, and never mind if she felt more than that for him. She was excellent in controlling her own feelings.

But she looked at the sleeping bags again and then mentally checked her pulse—that barometer was inevitably reliable. Her beat kicked in at just past "wary" and not quite "pending storm." Nothing in a couple of air mattresses intrinsically implied anything intimate. Unfortunately, any image that even remotely allied sleeping and Sam simply did. "You fibbed to Harry," she accused him.

"Yup. I learned that lesson from you," Sam said lightly, and grinned. "You like my surprise, don't you?"

She pushed back her hair, totally perplexed.

"I figured you would. I mean, you pretty clearly like outdoor stuff." He shrugged self-consciously. "I'll be the first to admit, I don't have the least idea how to set up a campout. You're talking about a kid who never slept outside in his life. But you told me how you usually spent your summer vacations, and I started to feel badly that you had this project foisted on you, and that maybe I could make it up to you a little if I—"

"Oh, Sam." The wary pulse died. She had the extraordinary urge to hug him. Not for the first time she noted the difference between him and other men she'd known. Sam had a fragile ego; he had a tough time owning up to his problems with reading and, man style, he was in no hurry to show weakness. But he'd never taken that ego out on her. He wasn't a man who used a woman, and she had to stop judging him the way she judged other men

"Come on," she said abruptly, and hurried for the door. "We've got to eat . . . and we need at least an hour before the sun goes down to find a place; we've got to change clothes, collect a few things—darnit, you've really never slept out under the stars?"

Sam let out a long mental sigh of relief before following her. It took very little to bring out that defensive blaze in her eyes, that certain tilt to her chin. A simple pink blouse could do it, for example.

While Harry and Leslie monopolized the dinner conversation he thought about that blouse. Harry had a highly imaginative story to tell about catching the trout that was their entrée. Les had scrubbed off her makeup and changed from her sexy open-weave sweater to a voluminous red sweatshirt, and was bubbling over with tales about the first fire she'd built, the first camping excursion she'd taken, her first mishap with a compass.

He couldn't take his eyes off her. He'd guessed the sleeping-bag idea would be touch and go, and truthfully had a few misgivings about it himself. He had to come up with something involving nature and exercise; he'd figured she couldn't turn down something she'd been promoting hell-bent for leather since she got here. Only the life experiences she took for granted, he simply hadn't had.

Ever since he'd met her, he'd been waiting for her to rub against those masculine insecurities, but that was turning into a double-edged sword. When he risked exposing himself as less than a man of the world, she came out of hiding—became warm like now, real like now, natural with him…like now. Her face was glowing with anticipation, her lips tilted in laughter. She couldn't stop talking and her eyes were as soft as melted chocolate.

At first glance, she was the last woman he'd want to show weakness to. Knowing her, he was coming to understand that she was the only woman with whom that was possible.

Leslie pushed back her chair and started gathering dishes in a clattering hurry. "Now, I don't want you worrying about us, Harry. We'll stay within calling distance of the house—"

"I still don't see that you two have to stay out there all night. Why don't you just come in after you teach him the stuff? It's going to get darned cold out there."

"And we'll probably end up back inside if it gets too cold." Leslie whirled on Sam. "You need a jacket, Sam. And a warmer shirt," she ordered him.

He made no effort to stop the whirlwind. Less than an hour later, she'd chosen the site in a cove of evergreens and put him to work making a ring of stones for a fire. The air bags had to be blown up—an exhausting task—and finding dry sticks for even a small fire wasn't that easy after the morning's drenching rain. She was fussy. Not only did the mattresses have to contain an exact amount of air for comfort, but he noted the precise, chaste distance she placed the sleeping bags from each other. And the business of making a fire . . . "You just can't ever do it carelessly, Sam. You have to consider wind direction, distance from the trees; you never risk anything catching fire that shouldn't. And all we want is a little something for warmth, so we're going to pack in the twigs like this—" She looked up suddenly, her eyes stricken. "Oh, God. I've been talking a mile a minute. Are you bored silly?"

She caught his slash of a smile. "Are you kidding? How am I going to learn anything if you don't teach me?"

"Well, I didn't mean to make all this sound like a lecture."

"You didn't, sunshine."

Silence fell between them like salve for a scald. Sam made being with him so easy. The last rays of sunlight had long since dropped behind the mountains. The Teton night was already growing cold. Their little fire snapped and crackled and over that orange glow Sam's eyes were the temptation of warmth. By firelight, his shaggy brows cast fierce shadows and his eyes had that soft silver of loneliness. His hair was wind rumpled, sand colored, thick. Hunkered down by the fire, his shoulders looked huge. The thought was fleeting, that those shoulders and arms could keep her warm if she just reached out . . .

She didn't, of course. She added another stick to the fire and brushed the bark dust from her hands. "I've never really asked you about your work."

He shook his head. "You really want to hear about probabilistic risk assessment?"

"Lord, no."

"Fusion research and development?"

"I can maybe handle multiplication tables," she offered wryly.

He chuckled. "Les, I've lived my work every day of my life; I don't need to talk about it the rest of the time."

She said carefully, "Your work's important to you."

"Of course it is. Just like yours is to you. But not now." He motioned to the treasure of stars just above their treetop shelter. They were close enough to touch. The night was close enough to touch. An owl hooted in the distance, and the scent of sweet pines melted with the distant rustling of animal sounds, primitive sounds. He could almost taste the smell of the burning wood, and he could touch the rich, dark earth. He couldn't remember a time when his senses had been more alive.

Except when he'd touched her. "Getting cold?" he asked her.

"A little. We should probably sack in..." She made a short trek into the woods, and when she returned she fussed a little with the fire and then settled on her sleeping bag to take off her shoes. "If it gets too cold, we can just head back to the house."

"Yes."

She took off her shoes and windbreaker, then slipped into her bag and zipped it up. She watched him then. He took off his shoes and socks first, then tugged off his sweater and wool jacket. Her heart started a peculiar rhythm when he finally dropped down to his sleeping bag and edged inside it. He should have kept on his sweater for warmth—she almost told him. She didn't; Sam might sleep best on the cool side. How could she possibly know how he was comfortable sleeping? And it wasn't her right to take care of him.

She curled up, her knees as close to her chin as the sleeping bag would allow. She always slept curled up. She didn't always sleep with a man two feet from her. His luminous eyes were on hers in the darkness and the smell of earth was all around her.

The firelight faded to embers that glowed in the night. Still she couldn't rest, even after Sam had closed his eyes and she heard his steady, even breathing. The quickened rhythm of her heart only gradually returned to normal. A tension in her shoulders that she hadn't been aware of slowly eased. Sam wasn't going to make a pass. Sam had never intended to make a pass. She'd been worried for absolutely nothing.

Later, just before her eyelids finally drooped down, she wondered vaguely if it was worry that had caused the tension. Or disappointment.

Moisture welled under her closed eyes. She didn't even know what the tears were for. In time, she slept.

Six

The nightmare had never been more than fits and starts of images for Leslie . . . a deserted wood hut shrouded and menacing by moonlight . . . the blur of a nameless boy's face on a hot summer night . . . The inside of the hut was mystically dripping with sharp icicles. She'd chosen to be there, but she was shivering and sick, inside, outside, all over, and the door to the hut had disappeared. She tried and tried so desperately to find a way out. Then, from nowhere—part of the dream and yet not—came Sam's sleepy, soothing voice, "Honey, it's freezing. Do you want to go up to the house?"

Vaguely she remembered answering "No" and snuggling back in her sleeping bag again. She wasn't

freezing or frightened; it was just night. She could
smell the rich, dark earth and hear Sam's even
breathing and feel all the luxury of being safe.

The next thing she was aware of was his husky
voice murmuring, "Wake up, Les."

She didn't want to, but her lashes fluttered once,
her eyes gazing on trees dripping with dew and the
grayness of pre-morning. Not an animal stirred, not
a leaf. Gradually, her senses registered that a warm
chest flanked her back, that Sam's arm was thrown
over her waist, that his whisper had been right next
to the shell of her ear. His closeness caused a spear
of panic that slowly ebbed as she fully wakened.

She had no memory of his moving his sleeping bag
next to hers. He'd unzipped both their bags halfway
to make the warmth of closeness possible. He'd
tossed the spare blanket over them and his shirt as
well. There was a reason why she'd slept so warmly,
why she still felt protected. She tested the fragile
sensation of trust. Sam could have taken advantage.
He hadn't.

"You're awake?" he whispered.

"Yes." It was only half a lie. If she were truly
awake, she would surely have had the sense to move
away. Instead she lay still, conscious of the weight of
his arm on her side, fathoming the nature of a man
who could make a harsh nightmare evolve into a
soft, mystical dream. The early-morning light was
unearthly, eerie. A faint silvery mist curled low to the
ground; they might have been enclosed in a cloud.

Gravity seemed suspended somewhere near the warmth of Sam's arm, the security of his chest against her spine, his breath at her nape.

She understood slowly why he'd wakened her. Above the silken haze shimmered the faintest lavender hue, and she could suddenly make out the outline of trees. Minutes passed—if time could be counted—but the medium of time seemed totally inessential. Color was everything. Lavender melted into pink; pink swirled with blue until the air was all pastels, soft like a hush, fragile as only a sunrise can be. Mountain peaks appeared between tree branches, bathed in color and iridescence. Drops of dew became jewels, some diamonds, some amethyst and amber and aquamarine.

"I've never seen anything like it," Sam murmured sleepily. "It's like . . . new. How can you not feel like something newborn when you see the beginning of a day like this?"

Yes. She felt just that way. Sleepy and young and new and coming to life; only that had much less to do with the beginning of a day than with the way Sam made her feel. Color was the feeling of sharing with him. Magic was something she could breathe. Wanting to believe came with the morning.

Sam's hand slid across her abdomen to her side, turning her flat on her back. His face was just above her. His tawny hair was rumpled from sleep, his dark eyes still had the glaze of dreams. The roughness of a night beard darkened his chin. Between them was

the twist and swaddle of bulky cloth—shirts, sweat-
shirts, sleeping bags—which made it awkward for
her to reach up and touch her lips to his.

If her kiss surprised him, it couldn't have surprised her more. She didn't exactly mean to; it just
happened. She kissed him because she wanted to put
a seal on their sunrise and if that wasn't logical,
then...it wasn't logical. For that one brief breath of
time she simply felt the fierce need to share. Loneliness was bigger than she was.

A dozen years of being alone poured into that kiss.
Her eyes closed, absorbing the texture of his smooth,
warm mouth. Her hands climbed his shoulders,
wound into his hair. She had to hold on to the feeling while she could; it would disappear, she knew,
like the colors of the sunrise. She had only a moment to claim that sensation of brand-new and fresh
and anything possible. Life and memories would in-
trude again, harsh and all too real. This wasn't life.
It was just...Sam. And a sunrise.

She knew no shame, not in that instant. She had
no memories of ever having touched a man before,
though she knew she had. She didn't want the memories. She just wanted...something. And she wanted
it so badly before it was gone.

"Easy, easy..." he murmured softly. She was as
restless and awkward as a kitten groping for a hold,
frantic for something secure...and he was right
there. She was so fiercely trying to get closer, and
only making the tangle of bedclothes worse. He cra-

dled her head in his hands, trying to soothe her. Her lips were warm satin, clinging as he'd only imagined they might cling to his, and where his thumb brushed her cheek he found the dampness of quick, helpless tears.

He couldn't fathom the tears, the embrace. He might have planned a morning kiss to blend with the sunrise, but not this. He wondered at the force of her dreams before waking, then didn't care. There wasn't time to question. He pushed at the barriers between them until the zipper of her sleeping bag gave, then his loosened as well. In some portion of his head he was trying to be careful. He didn't want her exposed to the chill of wet ground; he didn't want her cold but there was no other way to hold her. Her wildness was too sweet, too fragile. At that moment he'd never felt more powerful as a man. She'd turned to him.

Where she'd claimed his mouth, now he claimed hers, kiss after kiss. Tongue touched tongue and a low murmur escaped her throat; her hands tightened in his hair. He slid his arms down her body, crushing her closer. She was still wearing clothes—all her clothes, too many clothes. Her jeaned leg nudged between his, which was enough to cause him torture. He wished he could believe that she knew what she was doing to him.

The morning air was so chill; in her head that cold mist of a nightmare was seeping closer, threatening to make the wonder, the magic, disappear. There were so many things she didn't want to remember.

Sam was so warm, and as if it were a dream, she had to hurry; he wouldn't be here if she didn't; he'd leave her if he knew certain things . . . But he didn't know, and for a moment she wasn't that Leslie. She was just young again and afraid again, and she'd never felt yearning like this.

The sweep of his hand took in thigh and hip, stole under her sweatshirt to her breast. Her breath caught on a cry she couldn't help. She needed to touch him back but her arms and legs were in the wrong place and she was in such a terrible hurry . . . She felt a fingertip on her lips and opened her eyes.

Sam's smile was grave, his whisper barely audible. "Go silk for me, love. Easy and slow and soft. Just let me love you. There's nothing to be afraid of."

"Sam—" She felt so helpless.

His mouth covered hers, and she no longer felt helpless but engulfed, surrounded in magic. Her breasts had never been touched, not the way he touched them. Her skin burned under his fingers, branded precious. She felt like Beauty wakened from the prick of a spindle; her senses had been sleeping forever and now came alive all at once.

She needed this man. She felt his lips at her breast, the wash of his tongue. She felt his fingers slide down her jeans zipper and his palm steal inside, and she arched for that intimate touch. Her body flushed with hunger. Only for him. Sam made her feel new, a woman born fresh when he touched her, a blank slate on which there was no copy.

"So sweet," he murmured. "So wild and sweet..."

She could feel desire claiming him, the heady scent of his wanting her. The lion in Sam was the sheath of power in tenderness. She craved the tenderness. She trembled for the lion.

"Love..." He made a rope of pearl kisses on her abdomen, then trailed up, pushing aside the sweatshirt he'd never taken time to completely remove so his lips could string more kisses on her collarbone, then her throat, her face. "I need to know," he whispered. "I need to know now, and no stories, sweet. If you haven't made love before..."

She barely heard him. For a moment his words didn't register...and then ice slammed against the heated blood in her veins. He thought her an innocent?

He wanted an innocent.

She jerked back from him, blindly pushing down clothes, pushing up clothes, shaking everywhere as she grappled away from him. A slash of bright sun— the sunrise had long since disappeared—and reality was an ice-cold morning. She caught the shocked determination in Sam's face when he tried to reach for her. She said something—an "I'm sorry" and then another "I'm sorry"—but all she could think of was what a fool she was.

Her bare feet tripped and bruised on stones and cold, damp earth. It wasn't far to the house. Sam called out; she didn't pay any attention.

She tugged open the back door and there was Harry, with a sweet good-morning smile, and a genial "Well now. You two fare all right on your night in the woods? Pierce pass all those night-focusing tests?"

"Yes," she told him, and kept on going, taking the circular steps upstairs two at a time. Her lungs hauled in great rushes of air when she reached the top, and then she surged past her room and locked herself in the bathroom.

She flicked the shower on hot and started peeling off clothes. Her movements were mindless, automatic. Steam billowed in moving clouds that whispered around corners and coated the mirror. She stepped into the shower and felt the scalding spray assault her bare flesh. He wanted someone good. He wanted someone pure and clean. He'd even assumed she was a virgin, in spite of everything she'd told him.

The bathroom was paneled in redwood; normally heat and moisture blended with the woody scent to make the most soothing of baths. Not now. She was twenty-nine. How dare he expect a virgin? But he did have a right to expect a woman who'd lived by a moral code that he could understand. He wasn't capable of making the kinds of mistakes she had. He deserved a woman who was good as he was—not a woman who could never seem to wash the old shame clean....

The water turned cold before she finally turned it off and reached for a towel. She rubbed her skin dry, wrapped one towel around her head and another around her body, then stepped out of the bathroom carrying her bundle of clothes. Her throat felt thick with relief when she saw no sign of Sam in the hall, but she could have guessed that kind of luck couldn't last.

He was propped on her bed with her pillow behind him, one booted foot on top of the covers and the other on the floor. He hadn't changed his clothes or bothered to button his shirt, and those fathomless gray eyes were waiting for her.

She tugged open a drawer, snatched up underpants and a T-shirt. "Yes," she agreed, as if they were already halfway through a conversation. "I owe you an apology. More than an apology. You have every right to be mad as hell. All I can tell you..." Behind the open door to the closet, she dropped the towel, and pulled on the T-shirt and then jeans. It took longer to get past the lump in her throat than it did to get clothes on and face him again. "Sam, I never meant to...tease you. I couldn't deny in a thousand years that I've flirted with men, but there's a difference between that and teasing. In my entire life, I've never initiated any sexual contact unless I intended to follow through." She said unhappily, "It matters to me that you believe that."

He took in her stark-white face and haunted bright eyes. She'd instinctively adopted a defiant posture with her hands propped on her hips, and he just as instinctively wanted to shake her. "I believe that. I could also care less. I want to know what happened."

"Nothing happened. I realized I was making a mistake—"

"No, you didn't, and nothing was a mistake. You cared, Les. I know exactly how much you cared when I touched you. Something made you bolt like a scared rabbit, and I want to know what it was—and I *don't* want to hear any more nonsense about the five thousand men you have in your life."

She turned away from him, her skin flushed as she rubbed the towel on her damp head with shaking fingers. He neither sounded angry nor cold, just...quiet. Too quiet. Like a lion waiting for his prey to make a vulnerable mistake. She could have told him he didn't have to wait; she'd been making mistakes since the day she was born.

"Look, I just can't handle a relationship right now," she said clearly. "That doesn't excuse what I did, or maybe what I led you to believe this morning, but—"

It was as if he didn't hear her. "Can't you trust me enough to tell me?"

She had to push the words past a new knot in her throat. "And there were men, Sam. Not five thousand and maybe not all that many so recently, but there have been men. I don't know how you ever got the impression that I was green as grass—''

''Who hurt you, sunshine?''

She reached for a brush and started attacking her hair. He wasn't going to listen. The damn man just didn't want to listen, and she wished he'd never started calling her that nickname. For some ridiculous reason, it always made her feel like crying. ''I think it would just be a good idea if I left. There's no reason for me to be here, not anymore. You're not one of my snot-nosed kids, Pierce; you don't need to be motivated and you're ten times smarter than I am. I can teach you the exercises; I can set you up with your own program. I was going to have to do that anyway at the end of three weeks.''

''No.'' It was the first time he'd moved since she'd come into the bedroom, and she froze when he vaulted off the bed. So quietly he moved, and suddenly he was standing behind her, his eyes meeting hers in the small round mirror above the French provincial chest. The contrast was what startled her. His eyes were gray steel, but when had her own ever looked so vulnerable? ''Try to leave,'' he said with a deliberate slowness, ''and see what happens.''

And then he was gone.

She could easily have left anytime over that next week. A little idle threat from Sam certainly didn't stop her. She did notice that the Jeep's keys were no longer tossed casually on the kitchen counter. In fact, the Jeep was no longer parked in sight, which struck her as humorous. Sam was more than slightly naive if he thought lack of transportation would have prevented her from departing if she'd wanted to.

His strategy didn't impress her, either. Sam, damn him, treated her like a fluff ball that would unravel if he raised his voice above a bedroom tenor. He was an angel when they worked together mornings. Flowers appeared magically in her room. One day when he hadn't been to town and there was no possible way he could have done it, she found a blouse on her bed. A powder-pink blouse with an inset of lace and a delicate frill on the sleeves. Another day she found a small vial of perfume that smelled like hyacinths. He dragged Harry into it—Harry took up eating yogurt and gave up cigars. One night the two men concocted a bean-sprout salad for dinner. She hated bean sprouts, but since they rashly assumed she liked anything "natural," she had to eat the whole thing.

Neither bean sprouts nor Sam's infernal gentleness nor realizing how painfully she'd fallen in love with the man kept her from leaving. All of those things were momentum to go. She stayed only because of something remarkably undramatic: Sam and mirrors. Toward the end of the second week they had the confrontation.

The exercise wasn't a new one by that time. Reading backward through a mirror was an excellent exercise for dyslexia; it forced concentration and a different kind of focusing and a different use of the eye muscles. Unfortunately, it also put printed material in Sam's hands. She'd expected that to be a crisis, but since he was so busy being saintlike, courteous, obliging and patient, she hadn't fathomed what form the crisis would take.

It was just before lunch on Friday when she brought out the mirror. He hadn't been at it for five minutes when he suddenly snapped the book closed. Tension filled the room like an oncoming storm. "You only need to do this for five more minutes," she said smoothly. "Sam, you're doing fine—"

"I'm not doing fine and this whole thing is asinine. You want to hear me read, Leslie?" He jerked the book open again, this time on his lap. Through gritted teeth he worked through one sentence and then another, stumbling here, halting there. He hadn't finished a paragraph before perspiration formed on his forehead, and the next thing she knew the book crashed against the wall with a resounding thwack. Sam shoved aside the chair and a very few seconds later she heard the slam of the front door all the way from upstairs—she could probably have heard the echo of it across the Tetons.

She sat absolutely still for all of three and a half seconds. Mr. Master Control had just had a temper tantrum. She'd seen lots of them in her time; she'd just never expected one from Sam. It was just about at that instant that she knew exactly why she hadn't left and wasn't going to leave until her full three weeks were up.

Hands slung in the pockets of her bright-yellow jeans, she wandered downstairs, humming for the first time in days. She found Harry on the back porch, preparing his rod and reel for the afternoon's fishing expedition. "I have a favor to ask," she confessed.

His blue eyes swung in her direction. "Anything. Just ask," he said gruffly.

"I need Pierce to go fishing this afternoon, if you know a place we can rent another couple of rods and reels."

He frowned, only for a moment. "No problem."

"Sam's the problem. He won't want to go. In fact, I doubt he'll even be in to lunch—"

She was wrong. He came in to lunch cool, calm, polite and quiet. He poured her herbal tea and he touched her shoulder casually in passing and that flare of rage might never have been—but he definitely didn't want to go fishing.

"Well, you're going," Harry said flatly. "She says the process of casting takes a special focusing muscle and I'm here to see that everything goes smooth here and the last thing you should be doing is giving our Leslie a hard time. If she wants you to cast a fly rod for a couple of hours, then you're damn—pardon, Les—darn well going to cast a fl—"

"We're not playing those games anymore." Sam might have said it to Harry, but his eyes were ice-cold on Leslie.

"See, Harry?" she said helplessly.

Sam's tone was angry. "Cut it out, Les. It's not going to work."

"If I can eat yogurt, you can damn well go fishing," Harry yelled, then rapidly amended, "Pardon, Leslie. Darn well go—"

"You want to talk, we'll talk. Believe me we'll talk," Sam said lowly.

"Yes," she agreed. "With Harry there."

He shook his head. "You're not a coward, Les. And it's past time we stopped playing games."

Another area in which he was terribly wrong about her. She was a terrible coward, and game playing had successfully protected her for years. Sam was in a mood to let off a little emotional steam, and just possibly he didn't have a small discussion about reading in mind. When a man needed to blow, he needed to blow, but obviously she could only let that happen in circumstances where she could channel the explosion. If he decided to wring her neck, he was going to have to do it in front of Harry. Leslie had far more sense than to walk in front of a frustrated lion alone.

Undoubtedly he gave in on the distinctly male principle that a battle lost was not the war. She didn't much care why he gave in as long as he did. Harry wasn't much of a one to fuss about atmosphere. He was glad of the company and maintained a steady, rambling monologue on the long walk to his private fishing spot. "You'd think no one had ever discovered it before, and I'm telling you, these trout are fighters. You got to give 'em a little play, reel in, let out, reel in, let out.... You've fished before, haven't you?"

"Lots of times," Leslie assured him.

"Don't be using the fake worm for bait, now. Take that bright spangled caterpillar of mine—you try that and I'll guarantee they'll jump for it."

She'd never guessed Harry had an ounce of poetry in his soul, yet his fishing spot was a delectable bit of poetry. His stream had a granite bed that danced like gold under a beating sun; evergreen-spiked mountains secluded the haven in privacy. The water dipped and flowed in sun-dappled coves, then wound around a miniature green canyon.

She was only distracted by the scenery for a moment, and then hurriedly crouched down next to the men and fishing gear. Harry had two rods and they fashioned a third with line strung on a willow stick, Tom Sawyer style. Since fishing was hardly her priority, she insisted on using the stick. Sam was unnervingly quiet, but he handled his line and bait as if he knew what he was doing.

"Okay now, you two all set?" Harry grinned as he gathered his tackle together, missing Leslie's startled look of surprise. "I won't be going far, now; you just call me if you need me, Les. And not that I'm not willing to share my exact spot with you, but . . ."

She'd forgotten that a true fisherman never gave away his own private gold mine, and watched as a whistling Harry ambled off. She masked her dismay at his desertion by putting her chin up and showing an incredible case of fishermanlike concentration. Besides, he'd just promised that he wasn't going far.

Too many trees made casting difficult but not impossible. Sam, two rocks down from her, cast like a pro. Silence poured between them like liquid uranium. Volatile was the sun-warmed day and the plunk of her line in the water, then his.

She balanced the line while she tugged off her sweatshirt, although she already knew that this ploy was useless. Sam was long past the point of being diverted by halter tops and cleavage, and not for the first time, she regretted falling in love with a man who was smarter than she was. She'd successfully fooled dozens of men over the years, with her cleavage, wanton reputation and brazen lies. There wasn't a man west of the Great Lakes who'd ever caught on but Pierce. Sam was really extraordinarily annoying.

He was also extraordinarily disturbing. His line whistled over her head when he cast again; she had the nasty feeling he thought she was the one about to be reeled in. She carefully waited until she was fairly sure he had a nibble before casually observing, "You've fished before."

"Yes."

"With your dad?"

His eyes leveled with hers. He wasn't exactly in a mood for idle chitchat, but then neither was Leslie. She pulled in her line, laid the makeshift fishing pole on the rock beside her and settled, Indian style, facing him. "We're going to talk about it," she agreed.

"You bet we are."

"You've been cheating," she said calmly. "And I should have known better than let you get a book in your hands to begin with. You had a little problem with that mirror exercise, and so you've blown it all out of proportion—"

"Leslie," Sam clipped out, "if you think we're going to talk about nothing but reading, you're dead wrong. If you want to start there—fine."

"We start there or we start nowhere, so you might as well spill it out," she encouraged cheerfully.

He hesitated, but not for long. "Spill what out? Until I actually picked up a book, I had some stupid idea all this exercise nonsense was going to make a difference. It isn't. You heard me reading. I sounded like a second-grade kid with skinned knees and a runny nose trying to sound out words."

She stayed calm. "You expected the world to turn around in a week and a half, Pierce. That was never going to happen. In three weeks, I can give you all the exercises and you've got two solid months to follow through with them. Those two months are going to make the difference—"

"*If* there was going to be any difference, it would have shown up to some extent by now. You forget— one thing I do have is a brain. I knew the minute I picked up that book—"

"Which was supposed to be for the mirror exercise only. I told you not to read."

"Lady," Sam said coldly, and his eyes flashed to hers like a mirror of silver, "there's a level where no one tells me what to do and that includes you. I'll be damned if I'm going to make a total fool out of myself in front of an international crowd, and all for some idiotic award I never asked for. Someone else can have it, and as far as learning to read, to hell with that, too. I've gone through thirty-four years damned successfully without Dick and Jane and Spot—"

"You've got a bite," Leslie mentioned cheerfully.

He said nothing, but the pull on his reel was unmistakable. A slash of iridescent silver surged from the water on a splash, then ducked again. The trout didn't yet know he was hooked.

Sam didn't yet know he was hooked, either. She watched his shoulders ripple with tension and his thighs tighten as he started reeling the beauty in. The wind tossed his hair; sunlight glowed on his face. She loved him so fiercely at that moment.

"You want that award so badly you can taste it," she said softly. "You've earned it, Sam. You've got every reason to be proud, and you're going to do beautifully reading that speech. You just have to give yourself a little time. You don't seriously think I'd give you the chance to be my first professional failure, do you?''

The damn woman would choose a time to argue with him when he had his hands full. He should have expected it—he *had* expected it—but he was in a temporary mess. The trout bucked and swirled and fought the hook. He could care less about the fish, but he didn't have much choice but to catch it—or lose Harry's rod to the stream. Beads of sweat formed on his brow as he fought the sleek, shiny demon.

"And as far as learning to read," Leslie said gently, "you've wanted to all your life. You've missed it all your life. You've been ashamed about it all your life, and you specialize in being too darned hard on yourself, Sam. You're a little too smart, so you expect you should be able to do everything better than normal people. Who do you think you are, judging yourself like that? Who told you you have to be strong all the time, perfect all the time? Human isn't a dirty word."

Finally, he managed to flip the trout onto the shore, and bent down to unfasten the hook. That small success gave momentum to reach for another, and his voice was suddenly as smooth and cool as the sunlit stream. "Lord, can you talk."

"Pardon?" She was expecting a show of temper, not lazy humor. And Harry would have died, watching Sam slip the eighteen-inch trout back into the stream. "Sam, did you hear one word I was saying?"

"Sure." He rubbed his hands on his jeans and stood up. Leslie was perched only a few feet from him; he ignored the temptation to bridge that distance. Touching her, he'd lose control. Her lips were too red and her skin too soft and she was so ready to run. "Sure I heard you," he repeated quietly. "Human isn't a dirty word. Some people are too hard on themselves. Some people might even think they have to be perfect before someone else can love and care about them. Some people are a little touchy about trust." His eyes seared hers. "So when are *you* going to learn all that, Les?"

"What? When am I...?" The jab had come from nowhere, and she abruptly felt confused. How had he managed to twist everything so fast? And he was wrong, so wrong. She was nothing like that, yet she felt a twist of pain as if he'd stabbed at an open sore. "We were talking about you," she said fiercely.

His voice vibrated with gentleness. "I'm in love with you, Les. And you'd never have gone to the trouble of preparing that nasty little lecture—you wouldn't be here at all—if you weren't in love with me."

"No." She surged to her feet.

"Who hurt you?"

The harsh words carried on the wind, stung her eyes. "No one. Nothing. You're only seeing what you want to see, Sam. You don't know me. And if you keep trying to carry this further. . ."

The bird would fly. She was already taking wing. She whirled around and stalked toward Harry. Sam watched the sway of her hips, her stubborn spine, the toss of gold in her hair with frustration. He guessed that to chase her was to lose her.

Only he'd seen that furious, soft, soft sheen of tears in her eyes. It had shaken her to the high heavens when he'd told her he loved her. He hadn't lost her yet. His heart badly wanted to believe he was gaining ground, but he only had a week with her left.

Seven

I confess, I never would have thought you were capable of this." As she firmly rubbed the ammonia-soaked paper towel on the window over the sink, Leslie flicked Sam another disbelieving sidelong glance. He was standing at the huge kitchen window overlooking the ravine. In the most violent of housekeeping traditions, he was vigorously attacking every dust mote, every smudge, every conceivable mar on the glass. And he was doing it in a starched white shirt, albeit one with rolled-up cuffs. "Sam, don't you think we've done enough?"

He shook his head. "My mother used to have a phobia about leaving a place a mess after a vacation."

"But Sam, Harry's going to be here for another two days to close down the cabin, and it's already in twice as good shape as when I got here. And we've both got to pack if we're leaving first thing in the morning—"

Sam was so busy spraying more ammonia that he couldn't even look at her. "Harry's likely to forget things like windows."

Leslie managed to stifle a laugh only by exerting an extreme force of will. The last she knew, Sam wasn't quite so fussy about a little dust. Now, though, he'd spent at least twenty minutes on the left corner of that window, and used more ammonia than a whole house of glass would require. She could be wrong, but she had the sneaky feeling Sam had never washed windows before in his life. "Need some help over there?"

"No!" He jerked around, his eyes narrowed with alarm. "I mean...no. You're finished with that one?"

She nodded, her head cocked curiously at his increasingly strange behavior. She'd expected a lot of things on their last afternoon together, but not this. "And the ones in the living room are done. If you think it's that important, I could start on the windows upstairs," she said politely.

"No." His eyes darted around the room. "The refrigerator, Les. There's a smudge on that door, see it?"

"No."

He gave her an exasperated look. "All right, then. You just sit down for a minute."

"Look, I could help you—"

"No, no."

"Or I could certainly start packing—"

"Stuart, would you just sit down and shut up for me? Please?"

And they said women were irrational. Leslie tossed out the used paper towels, washed her hands and reached for the hand cream on the counter, making a mental note to remember to pack it. After that, she obediently sat down on a kitchen chair and crossed her jean-clad legs at the ankles.

Sitting down, she discovered, was a mistake. She immediately had nothing to do but look at Sam, which was exactly what she'd been avoiding for the entire week. She studied him with broody possessiveness. His hair was rumpled and getting shaggy at the back; his skin was wonderfully sun-bronzed. Jeans suited his long legs perfectly, and if she couldn't fathom why he was back in a starched white shirt, there was no question that his shoulder muscles had been toned and honed over three weeks of exercise. She thought, I've done that much. He's healthier and he knows what the sun feels like on his face. And at least . . . I never hurt him.

All week he'd given her incredible opportunities to hurt him. He wanted her as a lover, she knew that. He'd stolen kisses and invented excuses to touch her. He'd hiked and climbed and swum with her. He'd shown her in a thousand ways that he respected her, cared for her, wanted her, and perhaps the most precious of all, trusted her.

He was so damned sure he had a good woman on his hands who only needed time and tenderness to be won over.

Sam was so foolish. He'd won her ages before—if not from that first kiss, then from the first time she'd met him and he'd been such an emotional, testy, hostile, distinctly *male* package of insecurity over having to admit to her he couldn't read. She adored the man, and falling in love for the first time at twenty-nine was a painful experience. She was awfully old to discover just how powerful the emotion was.

Her love was strong enough that she wanted to protect him from getting involved with the wrong woman—her. The day they'd been fishing, he'd shaken her badly. Sam had turned her words about people making mistakes against her, and for one brief moment she'd been tempted to spill everything to him. She knew that he was asking her to. He wanted her to believe that she could trust him, that he wouldn't judge her, that he wouldn't think the less of her because she'd made a past mistake or two.

She believed that he would try.

She thought that, in his head, he might even succeed. But in his heart he'd never feel the same way about her if he knew what she'd done. If she couldn't forgive herself, how on earth could she expect him to forgive her?

She'd protected both of them by keeping her distance, but somehow she'd expected something a little different from Sam this last late afternoon than washing windows. "Sam?" she murmured.

"Hmm?"

"I swear to heaven that spot has to be clean. There couldn't be anything out of that specific view that you wouldn't want me to see, now, is there?"

"Lord, you're suspicious." He peered out one last time, then tossed down his towel with a sigh of relief. "We can go outside now," he announced.

"We couldn't before?" She obediently stood up.

"I didn't say that." He started rolling down his cuffs.

"There's some reason why we need to go outside?"

His dark eyes pounced on hers. "I've never been through a half hour like this last one. And if you ask even one more question, I may turn you over my knee," he said darkly.

"I'm shaking, Sam. Really shaking." She added, "The left side of that window is incredibly clean. You could hire out as a window washer for left sides. Lots of people probably don't care if the whole window gets cl—"

She felt a distinctively sharp pat on her fanny, followed by another and another. About the time they were out the door, he'd stopped patting and simply circled her neck in a gentle but unmistakable stranglehold. His face was so close, for that moment. So close, so dear, so familiar, so...wanted.

"For God's sake, say something about the tie," he whispered, and only reluctantly released her when they'd reached the patch of grass by the ravine.

Harry was waiting for them, his hair slicked back and a bow tie on his plaid shirt. A red sheet had been stretched out as a tablecloth, and he'd used his precious fishing bucket to chill two bottles of champagne. Wildflowers had been jammed in a water glass in the center of the sheet, steaks were ready to put on the fire, and a huge Leslie-style salad was waiting to be served. Harry had arranged everything but the silken early-evening breeze and soft sunlight, both of which came free. His face fell four feet when he saw tears fill Leslie's eyes.

"Harry! What have you two done?" She surged forward, and with a smoke-edged laugh bent down to kiss his bright cheek. "All this. Good heavens, even champagne! And flowers—"

"I just figured it'd be less to clean up if we ate outside this last night," Harry said gruffly. "Didn't go to any special trouble."

"A wonderful salad, and steaks. And Harry, I *love* your tie..."

Sam reached for the champagne, watching her gradually reduce Harry from acting like a grown man to behaving like a fourteen-year-old with a crush. The cork popped with an explosion, flying high in the sky, and foam bubbled out over his wrist. Absentmindedly he licked at the residue, not able to take his eyes off her.

Sunshine was tangled in her hair; her lips were curved in laughter. Her long slim legs were accented by jeans and her white top showed off satiny golden skin and the warmth of her. His eyes snapped a mental picture and framed it for tomorrow. And after tomorrow.

He couldn't imagine ever wanting, needing, loving another woman the way he did Les.

Despair was like a live ache inside him. It wasn't over, not for him. Florida to Minnesota was a bridgeable distance. The differences in their careers was a technical problem that he'd already mentally solved. He could always teach arithmetic in Minnesota. Heaven knew, he was qualified. Assuming, of course, that he could ever make her see the possibilities, and that was exactly where despair kicked in.

She'd made him jealous, frustrated, furious, touchy and exasperated. She'd aroused his passion to a screaming level and she'd taught him to fib. She'd taught him emotions. He loved her with a fierceness that he'd never fathomed having for anyone, but he didn't know how to get her to take that love. Nothing he knew how to do as a man had made any difference.

Harry was fretting. "Suppose I should have gotten some fancy glasses, but there just wasn't much of anything in the house but these old things."

"They're perfect, Harry." Sam handed her the water glass half filled with champagne. The bubbles spit and whistled as she took that first sip.

"After this assignment, I retire, you know. Heck, I was already more than semiretired when I took this job."

Leslie smiled at him. "Then we'll have to toast your having lots of long fishing days ahead."

"Sure enough." He clinked glasses with her, and then with Pierce. They all took a small sip.

"Another toast," Sam suggested. Both sets of eyes turned to him. He looked only at Leslie. "We'll toast . . . your winning," he said softly.

"Winning what?" Harry questioned.

"You won what you wanted to, didn't you, Les?"

"Yes." She met his brooding eyes over the glass. Her own glance dropped. She took one quick gulp of champagne, then another, and had to pray the smooth, fruity wine would go past the sudden lump in her throat.

It was long after midnight and the house was finally quiet. The two bottles of champagne were gone; dinner had ended hours before in a firelit game of three-man gin rummy. Though Sam had gone off on a long walk alone, Leslie had heard him return and climb the stairs to his room almost an hour before.

Alone behind her closed bedroom door, she viewed the open suitcase on her bed as if packing were the only thing on her mind. She laid her jeans in first, then silently wrapped her shoes in bags and tossed them in, then lingerie. Lips compressed, she chose a sundress and jacket for traveling tomorrow, mulled what cosmetics she should lay on top, and then started reaching for blouses to fold.

Her suitcase was nearly full when she reached for the only hanging item left in the closet, the pink blouse with the inset of lace in the shape of the cameo that Sam had given her. She folded it with meticulous care, barely aware of what she was doing. For that matter, if anyone had asked her anything about what she'd done in the past half hour, she doubted she could have told them. Her hands obediently picked up and folded and packed and smoothed and did what they had to do. Her mind was in an entirely different world.

When she had finished packing, she checked the room and discovered that she'd missed a scarf dropped near the foot of the bed. Methodically she folded that, too, quietly opened drawers one last time to make sure she'd left nothing else, and then it was done.

With the same calm precision she'd done everything else, she switched off the light and slowly removed her clothes. Her jeans were tossed on top of the suitcase, then her white top. An ounce of lace underpants was last, and when she was bare in the darkness she took a long, slow breath.

Her pulse announced that she was about to have a heart attack.

On bare feet she padded across the carpet and silently opened her door. Not a sound or light disturbed the upstairs, or the down. Sam's door was slightly ajar; it made no sound when she opened it and glided stark naked inside.

His windows were open, and a night breeze fluttered the curtains. Sam was turned toward the wall, a still, long bundle of man in the darkness, very much asleep. She hesitated for a long moment, took a step toward him and then hesitated again.

Sometimes a woman had to make a decision that was dangerously unwise.

From the moment he'd toasted her "winning," she knew she was coming in here. It had nothing to do with her and everything to do with Sam. Her head had done a rationally good job of talking her out of this. Her heart had insisted that she had no other choice. Sam was not a man who showed vulnerability easily; he'd risked his ego and pride in admitting to loving her. She just couldn't leave with him thinking he'd failed at something that important to him as a man.

This night, she wanted him to feel that he'd won everything that mattered to him. She couldn't leave...believing she'd hurt him.

She slid closer to the bed, and soundlessly bent down to push aside enough covers to make a space for herself. Her fingers had barely touched the blanket before Sam whipped around, a startled scowl arched between groggy dark eyes. He lurched up on an elbow while she silently cursed the man for being such a restless sleeper.

"Les? What on earth are you—?"

"Shh."

The room was ink black. He'd wakened from a panic dream in which Les was gone from his life. The last thing he was prepared for was her smooth, bare leg kneeling next to his, her pushing aside the covers, her kneeling over him to press a kiss on his heartbeat. The air rasped out of his lungs in one shocked breath. After that he gave up breathing altogether.

Her lips skimmed his body the way a sailboat dips and soars for waves. She kissed his throat, his abdomen, his throat, his shoulders. With a slowness she hoped was maddening, her fingers whispered over his flesh, seducing with all the tease and promise of woman.

She moved like a slow, sensual phantom in the darkness. She knew exactly what she was doing, exactly what she wanted him to feel. She rubbed her cheek on his chest; she let her hair tickle and scrape against his flesh; she slid the tips of her breasts across his hair-roughened skin. She caressed him intimately, wantonly wooing his hardness, his desire. Only darnit, she was trembling like an earthquake.

"Leslie . . ."

"Let me," she whispered fiercely.

Her mouth covered his, making it impossible for him to say anything. Her tongue shivered between his teeth, searching out his warm wetness and the intimate touch of tongue to tongue. He tasted like sleep and champagne.

He tasted like the man she loved. And her big plans to seduce him, her ardent wish to just this one night be the lover he wanted, vanished like a shiver of wind. She abruptly felt as stable as a feather.

Sam loosely pinned her leg as he gently rolled her on her back. His fingers threaded through her hair. The wind had died outside; the clouds had moved past the moon. He studied her eyes by moonlight, her trembling mouth, the fragile whiteness of her face. "I thought I was dreaming you," he said softly.

She shook her head.

"I've imagined you naked beside me. I've imagined taking you a hundred times." She tried to lift her face, to mold her mouth on his so he couldn't talk, but he wouldn't let her. "I dreamed of what it would feel like inside of you. I dreamed of making love to you over and over until you knew, Les, until you were absolutely sure that you could trust me, that I loved you, that I would never hurt you."

She shook her head again, not in denial of what he was saying but in denial of what he wanted: a future. She touched his cheek, not wanting to hurt him, having to. "Sam, please don't want me to lie to you. This can only be for tonight."

His smile was grave. "If that's what you really think, love, you made a very bad mistake when you came in here."

She didn't understand what he meant, and then his mouth claimed hers. In a moment, the stars outside came in. He'd never kissed her like that before, like a man who would brand her with his mouth. Her head sank back into the pillow, her eyes shuttering closed as she felt the force and potency of his hunger.

She'd unleashed the lion.

At that instant she understood the depth of her mistake, but it was too late. His mouth only left hers to stalk the vulnerable parts of her body. She expected his kiss on her breasts, but not the lash of his tongue igniting pinpoints of hot yellow fire on her skin. She expected his patience and control. She expected a gentle, quiet buildup to intimacy.

Instead, he teased where she was vulnerable and he did it deliberately. Slowly, he turned her over and kissed her fanny and let his tongue count her vertebrae. Slowly, he turned her back and slid her on top of him where he could bury his face in her breasts. She suddenly didn't have the strength of cotton and her heart was pounding and then she made another mistake, in locking her legs together. It wasn't a conscious choice, just old instincts of self-protection, yet Sam suddenly trailed his lips down and then down again. His kisses traced the line where her legs were clamped together; his palms stroked and smoothed, trapping her into relaxing.

A tremor drove up her spine when she felt his lips where his lips shouldn't be. She wasn't prepared for the wash of sensations that ricocheted through her in splashes of sharp, bright yearning. She thought she knew so much about sex. She hadn't known a woman could die from wanting. And when her skin had a silk sheen of moisture, when her breath was coming in frantic gasps, his mouth climbed back up to hers again to sap the last of breath and sanity from her.

He wanted her fear. She understood it suddenly. He was courting the trembling, the unsureness, the too-awkward, too-desperate need. Only this time, she badly didn't want to feel like brand-new and young; she wanted to be Eve for him, a skilled Eve who could please her mate. She wanted to be sultry and wanton and bold. Not shy.

She felt his finger sliding inside her and curled around him as if she could bury herself in Sam, his smell, his warmth, his arms. He just held her close for that moment, both of them out of breath, and then he murmured, "You know exactly what I'm going to do to you?"

"Sam—"

"You know," he whispered. "Just like you knew when you walked in here that there was no way in hell I'd leave it at one night. I'm coming after you, Les.

I'm going to be there and I'm going to love you, and there's nothing—nothing—you can do to stop me."

"Sam—"

His mouth sealed hers still as he moved over her. A cry shuddered from her lips when she felt his slow intimate intrusion. Her legs instinctively tightened around him, earning her kisses all over, on her throat and lips and cheeks. "We're going slow," he whispered, "because I don't give a damn what you think you know. And we're going slow, love, because I'm going to do my damndest to drive you mad."

She was a candle flame, flickering and fragile and bright for Sam's match. One moment he covered her; one moment he buried himself inside her and the fire was a fierce agonizing burn of pleasure. And then he withdrew, and there were sweet, soothing kisses and nothing she could hold on to. He repeated the sequence, and repeated it again, until her hands were clutching for him and her whole body felt the glaze of heat.

"Don't do this to me!" Her rage was barely an audible murmur.

"Tell me what you want."

"Stay. Stay with me; stay inside me..."

She couldn't wrap her legs around him tightly enough; she couldn't breathe or think. He started a fierce, driving climb that refused to end and he kept whispering to her, coaxing sweet murmurs that made her skin flush and her pulse pound. The darkness was nothing but Sam; there was nothing to cling to but Sam. She was turning into fire, burning up, every cell in her body coiling up to spring...

His mouth sealed her fierce cry between them. Tears sprang under her closed eyelids. And Sam just kept holding her, rocking her softly, long into the night.

The buzz came from a distance. It was just enough of a noise to stir Leslie from a deep sleep but not enough to make her want to waken. She never wanted to wake up again. Sam had barely let her sleep all night and now she had them settled perfectly, his rough chin to her temple, her breasts to the warmth of his chest, his leg straddling hers. He was far too heavy and far too warm and this was exactly how she intended to sleep for the next hundred years...

Except that the bee kept buzzing. Her alarm clock, she realized gradually. Her plane was leaving at eight and the alarm had been set for six. Her groggy eyelids jerked open.

"It'll go away," Sam murmured. "Ignore it, sunshine."

Her body wanted to. Her body craved sleep and Sam—not necessarily in that order—and he didn't make it easy for her to untangle herself from that warm haven. Cold morning air attacked her bare flesh when she stood up. Sanity was just that cold.

"Don't go." His dark eyes were wide-awake, as if he'd never slept at all. They were the exact color of temptation.

"I have to," she said swiftly.

"No, you don't."

His eyes could almost make her believe that. She stumbled out of the room, fast, and headed for the bathroom, praying that a hot shower would jolt some sense into her.

The pelting spray made her conscious of private places where she felt tender, places she'd never expected to be tender. The water erased none of the night's memories and none of the temptation to stay with him. Sam was the one who'd washed her clean the night before. Like a tidal wave she'd felt the power and wonder of a woman loved. She'd had no name in the darkness, no history. Loving him had been as natural as air, sunshine, rainbows.

She flipped off the shower and roughly toweled herself dry. In the mirror over the vanity, the same Leslie unfortunately showed up: a woman who not only had a history, but a past that didn't include sunshine and rainbows. And if the man loved her, she knew exactly how much more she loved him.

When she crossed the hall, she could hear Harry fussing down below in the kitchen. The aroma of fresh coffee floated up the stairs. Sam was waiting in her room when she rushed in for her clothes. He'd thrown on jeans but nothing else, and his eyes had lost none of that brooding temptation he'd had when she'd left him in bed.

She dropped the towel, drew on underpants, and reached for the sundress and jacket she'd laid out the night before. In a few seconds, she managed to force a flow of quiet words past the lump in her throat. "You follow those instruction sheets I gave you. And you remember what I told you—that you'll see improvement and then it'll seem to stand still. No giving up, Sam. But no pushing the exercises either; and I know darn well you'll try to push them...."

"I want you to go with me to Rome."

She shook her head, a difficult thing to do when she was trying to brush her hair at the same time. He smiled and stole the brush from her hand.

"Harry's waiting downstairs," she protested. "I have to go..."

His mouth smoothed over hers. It wasn't the kiss of a man who sought to dominate but the caress of a sunrise—all color and softness and dreams. Her arms circled his neck before she could stop them. His lips lingered on hers and all she could think of was memorizing the taste, touch, feel, scent, sound of him.

"I need you," he said softly.

"No."

"No," he agreed. "We won't talk about that kind of need, and we won't talk about how you feel and I feel. We'll make it much more simple, Les. I need you to come with me to Rome, to be with me there. I can't do that without you.''

She stepped out of his arms, feeling impossibly confused. She tossed her brush in the bag, closed the suitcase and lifted it. He was still standing there. She'd never expected the subtlety of a silken trap.

Rationally, she knew he was only inventing an excuse to pursue their relationship. Emotionally, she knew exactly how sensitive he was about that conference in Rome, how afraid he was of exposing his failure to read in front of his colleagues. Her mind flashed images of his facing that, alone.

I can't do that without you.

Damn the man.

"Will you?" he murmured.

"Yes," she snapped, and rushed for the stairs before she could say or do anything else she knew she'd regret.

Eight

Nine hours on a jet were enough to make Leslie's knees wobbly and her stomach feel like an exhausted jumping bean. In the process of walking down a corridor, she won three whistles, one blown kiss and two unmistakable propositions that required no translation from Italian into English. Customs was a gauntlet of dark-eyed men who assumed she wanted to be affectionately pinched while they went through her luggage.

Blondes were obviously at a premium in Rome. If Sam didn't find her soon, she was going to hide in the women's room.

Minnesota was all cool greens in August. Rome was a shock of hot-white sunshine, unbearable heat and too many men. Leslie lifted the collar of her blouse, horrified at the dampness on the nape of her neck. She was wearing Sam's pink blouse, a pale gray linen skirt and matching sandals. The skirt was new; she'd had nothing in her closet to match the blouse. It was the first time in her life she'd shopped for anything with a demure, tasteful, understated, calm image.

She felt about as calm as a cat being fried for breakfast. And demure? How in hell was she ever going to be able to pull that one off? This effort was all a waste, anyway. Her hair was already bouncing in abandoned curls, moisture was collecting behind her knees and neck, and exhaustion had erased her courage. There was no possible way she belonged in Sam's world.

"Lord, you look delectable, Les."

She whirled and was immediately caught up in soft dark eyes and Sam's lazy smile. Then his warm lips gave her just a quick kiss. A possessive kiss. Quakey knees became quakier. They weren't supposed to start out this whole thing with kisses. "I was afraid you wouldn't be able to find me in this crowd."

"You have to be kidding." He grabbed her suitcase and tucked her tote just above it so he had a free hand to connect with the small of her back. His grin was mischievous. He looked strong and tall and confident. Not at all like a man who desperately needed her help. "Terrible flight?"

"Just long." He was propelling her past glass doors, and suddenly the humidity of close bodies inside the airport became the bake of a sun there was no hiding from. Rome smelled . . . different. Foreign and exciting and terrifying. Like a place where she definitely didn't belong.

"I've been here two days, so I can fill you in on the ropes. Never count on an elevator working; assume the entire city will close down between noon and three; and if you put your shoes outside your hotel-room door at night, they miraculously return shined in the morning."

He was still talking as he hailed a taxi. The vehicle looked marginally pre-World War II and was coming at them as if the driver hoped for a head-on collision. One screech of brakes later and Sam was handing her into the back seat. The driver must have been native. His eyes poked holes where her skirt had ridden up on her thighs, and that condition had only existed for a millimeter of a second before she discovered it.

"And I've mastered the language," Sam continued as he slammed the car door and gave the now innocent-faced driver their address. "You only need one word to get along here, Les, maybe two. *Prego* is the critical one. You say *prego* and smile at the desk clerk, and he instantly produces your room key. You say *prego* and hand over a coin to the man in front, and he produces a taxi out of thin air. . . ."

"*Sam*." She'd never heard him talk so much, or so fast, and he was eating her up with his eyes.

"You wore the blouse," he said with satisfaction.

"Yes." Her nerves all collected in a little dry ball in her throat. And why was she the one out of breath when he was the one talking a mile a minute?

"Do you want to know what the other critical word in the language is?"

She gave up. "Tell me."

"Gelati."

"Which means?"

"I can't tell you what it means until you tell me how tired you are. Jet lag? Starvation?"

"Yes, and yes."

"Will they wait for one short half hour?"

She had in mind a cheerful hello, a careful treading of tactful waters, an establishing of acceptable distance between them. Sam was treating her as if he'd just gotten his first puppy.

At his direction the taxi whisked past the Fountain of Trevi, St. Peter's and the catacombs. The shaded city park appeared from nowhere. Sam paid the driver a handful of lira to wait, and as fast as she was standing on the brick sidewalk he deserted her.

Children were racing and tossing balls. Family clusters were laughing beneath huge old shade trees that, if they didn't dispel Rome's summer heat, blocked the ceaseless sun. There was a concession in the middle of the park, from which Sam emerged with two ice-cream cones. *"Gelati,"* he explained, and gave her enough time to take a first lick before mentioning, "Forget butter pecan. Forget even chocolate mint. Are we moving to Rome or are we moving to Rome?"

Her teeth sank into the delectable cold ice cream but her eyes were on Sam. Her pulse ruthlessly informed her that she hadn't come here to help him but rather because she couldn't face not seeing him one last time. She tried to ignore that pulse. "I'm not sure it would be a rational decision to move to Rome for ice cream."

"Rational?" He waved the comment aside with a flip of his hand. "This is worth killing for."

"Yes."

"You look beautiful, sunshine."

"Sam?" She moved her fingers in front of his eyes, just to make sure someone was home upstairs. "The conference? Your reading? Schedules? Hotel accommodations?"

He leaned over and kissed her. By the time he'd finished, ice cream was melting from the cone onto her fingers and they'd attracted several approving onlookers. American tourists were not necessarily popular everywhere; lovers were always welcome in Rome.

Having experienced the time change himself, Sam was aware that Leslie was exhausted, disoriented and a little overwhelmed. Not that it was gentlemanly to hit a lady when she was down, but he made sure she was more exhausted, disoriented and overwhelmed long before he checked her into the hotel, collected her room key and steered her toward the open lift. "There's only two things I can't get out of," he admitted wryly.

"Yes?" Her eyes were so groggy she couldn't see straight.

"The speech thing tomorrow night. And the evening after that, I seem to have put myself on the spot. Brooks seemed to feel . . . I told you about Brooks?"

She touched her fingertips to her temples. She thought so. Brooks was some American mathematician who was part of the American delegation representing the U.S. at the conference.

"Brooks suggested I put together some kind of get-together the night after tomorrow. French, Russian, German, American mathematicians—there's one Japanese man. We're all in the same field, Les."

"How many?"

Sam steered her out into the third-floor corridor. "Thirty or forty, I guess, if they bring their wives. Anyway, do you think I should have food?"

Leslie resisted the urge to take off her shoes and stumble blindly down the unfamiliar hall toward the nearest bed. "Food?"

"Food. Drink. I figured you'd know. I asked them up to the suite around seven, but then Brooks started talking about how we were representing Americans and American hospitality and . . ."

She stopped dead. "Sam? You asked forty people over two days from now without making any catering arrangements with the hotel?"

He twisted a key in a lock and pushed open a door. "See? I told you I needed you." He swung her luggage up on a canvas shelf and moved ahead of her into the room to close the drapes.

The bedroom was old and elegant, decorated in a muted rose with dark wood accents. A long marble table flanked a low couch under the window. A huge vase of bougainvillea scented the room from the dresser and next to it was a crystal bowl overflowing with fresh fruit. All Leslie really saw was the double bed. And the pillows. Lord, they looked soft.

"Now, through here—" he opened a door "—is the rest of the suite: a living room, where I've got my computer and work set up, and then another bedroom and bath. All you have to do is knock on the door if you need anything. Believe me, I'll hear you."

His hands closed on her shoulders. The faintest pressure and she was sitting on the bed, looking up at him blankly. He knelt down, took off her shoes. She reached for some semblance of awareness. "Your reading? You haven't told me how—"

"Terrible," he said blithely. "Thank God you're here, sunshine." He reached behind her to plump up the pillow, and then pulled down the spread.

"On the phone, you sounded so worried about the speech. And until then, I thought everything was going so well for you—"

Which she'd needed to think or Sam had known damn well she would have changed her mind about coming. He unclipped the belt from her waist, and watched her eyes blink open, but she didn't really protest.

"Sam?" For some reason he was pushing her. And then her cheek sank into the pillow. "We'll find a way for you to manage that speech," she promised him wearily. "And I'll organize something for your mathematicians. You don't have to worry about anything. I'll..."

"Yes. You can start bossing me around just the minute you wake up," he murmured. "I was counting on you to arrange everything, Les."

Leslie's palms were slick when she entered the tall, arched doorway of the ballroom the next night. Sam's hand at her back didn't help the tangle of nerves that was turning her spine rigid.

The people who flooded toward Sam spoke variations of English, with a Russian, Spanish, Japanese, French, or occasionally an Italian accent. They all knew him or his work, and Sam was totally at ease with his colleagues. She had thought he needed someone he knew and who cared about him beside him to give him confidence.

It didn't take her five seconds to realize that she didn't fit and would never fit in his world. She knew how to hold her own in a group of normal men, but these weren't normal men; they were brains, like Sam, born to privilege and choices. Sam needed a lady at his side who was born a bastard in a backwater town like he needed buckteeth.

The kind of woman he needed was everywhere, dressed appropriately in navy, white, or black. Not emerald green. The dress Leslie had taken hours to choose was all wrong—green was too bright. She'd deep down known it was too showy, but this was a celebration for Sam and she thought the happy color appropriate. It wasn't. No shoulders were showing but hers. Attire was formal, but dowdy dress was the rule of the evening and she clearly stood out like, well, the wrong kind of woman.

Sam had said she looked wonderful but Sam was blind. From the time he met her, he'd been determined to be blind about her. She never thought, however, that he would lie to her as well. When he stood up on that podium, one could have heard a pin drop in a room of some five hundred people. When he gave that speech, she could have died of pride. His colleagues stood in tribute paying applause at the end, a measure of the respect he'd earned worldwide. Emotional tears filled Leslie's eyes...but so did shock. He hadn't read the speech. He'd memorized it...and delivered it without hesitation. He didn't need her. He'd never needed her.

Sam answered the suite's living-room door for the third time and worried what was keeping Les. She'd left him more than an hour before...or tried to. She'd kept thinking of another instruction she had to give him before their little party started. "Watch the wine, Sam. Call down for more *before* you see you're getting low, and if that isn't enough food... Sam, didn't your dad ever teach you how to tie a tie...? Did we turn the air conditioning up? If there are a lot of smokers, Sam, turn it up again and..."

He told her, "Yes, yes and yes" and reveled in all her bossing. She'd been too quiet all day, not like

Les. And though he figured an hour wasn't an unreasonable time for her to change clothes, he was sure she'd be back here long before the people started arriving.

Six filled the room and then ten. By eight o'clock, more than forty people were crowding every corner of the suite. The flowers, wine and canapés she'd somehow arranged for were either being admired or devoured but she still wasn't there.

He slipped out into the hall rather than use the connecting door to the suite, a frown pleating his brow as he rapped on her door. "Les? You're all right?"

"Sam!" Her tousled head appeared while the rest of her hid behind the door. He understood why, when he realized she was wearing a white silk robe and nothing else. "What on earth are you doing here?" she scolded. "For heaven's sake, you're hosting a party in there—"

He stalked in and closed the door. His eyes narrowed. He hadn't seen that certain defiant tilt to her chin or the streaks of gold when her head tossed just so in weeks. "What are you talking about? Why aren't you dressed?"

"I was never going," she informed him calmly. "I set it up for you—you needed that. But for heaven's sake, Sam, you don't need me there. Those people want to talk to you and I'd just be completely in the way."

"That's the most ridiculous thing I've ever heard of." He crossed the room in a flash to open her closet door, and grabbed the first thing he saw. It was black and silky and looked distinctly Les.

She took it from his hands and hung it back up. "No!"

"There's no way in hell I'm going back to all those people without you," he said flatly.

"That's ridiculous! You're perfectly comfortable with all of them."

"No, I'm not. I'm miserable. So what's wrong with this?" He tugged out something bright pink; she snatched it out of his hands.

"Everything!" She hung that one back up too. For one stark instant he saw the vulnerable misery in her eyes, all the white tension around her mouth. And then her chin soared up again. "Look, Sam—"

"If you're not going back with me, I'm staying here with you." He added thoughtfully, "We could take a carriage ride by moonlight around the Colosseum. Want to do that?"

"No." She looked frantically at the connecting door to the suite where party sounds were seeping through. "Sam, that group is important to you, and they're all going to be wondering where you are. You have to go back in there—"

"When you're dressed, we will."

"I can't." She had to rush to get in front of him before he took apart the rest of her closet. "Sam, I can't," she said desperately. "Don't you understand? You look at me, but you're just determined to see someone I'm not. I don't fit in. I don't even have the right things to wear. I'd embarrass you—"

"Ah." Not for the first time since he met her he was tempted to shake her. Instead he lifted her arms to his shoulders and homed in—not easy to do when she was shaking her head—on her lips. She turned still as stone and he could feel how cold her body was. He warmed her, slowly, with kisses she was trying to tell him she didn't want and with hands tenderly roaming her flesh through the silk of her robe. "Damn fool woman," he whispered softly. "Who would have guessed you were insecure about anything, sunshine?"

"I'm not insecure. I'm realistic," she tried to tell him.

"Realistically, you shine wherever you go. How could you be so silly? You're beautiful. I can't help it if you make all the other women look like tuna fish to your caviar."

The analogy was so horrible that she almost made the mistake of smiling. "Sam—"

"Now, I know a gathering like that is boring for you but we can get rid of them in an hour. At most, two." He kept one arm on her shoulder when he reached into her closet again. Blindly he pulled out something—a pink blouse. When she didn't instantly panic, he dropped his other hand from her shoulder, taking her silk robe down with him. There was some kind of cleaning tag on the garment. He removed it, which gave him something to do besides react to her standing in front of him in nothing but a pair of pants and bra.

"Remember the day I told you I couldn't read? I never thought I could do that, Les. For thirty-four years, I'd never told anyone and I wasn't about to start with you. Everyone's got something they're a little sensitive about—"

"I'm not oversensitive about anything. You're determined to misunderstand this—"

"You're probably right," he said smoothly. He threaded one blouse sleeve over her arm and then the other, then pushed her head to his chest so he could start on the buttons at the back. "I guess I'm the only one who ever gets hung up on what other people think, other people's judgments. Right, love?" She kept trying to move her head. Buttoning a woman's blouse was hard enough without her fidgeting. "Luckily, you taught me something about two against the world, Les. And that no one else's judgments ever did matter a hoot in hell." He stood back, turned her so he could critically judge his buttoning job and ignored her soft brown eyes helplessly zoned on his. "I think we're going to have to do a little better than this," he said matter-of-factly. "Not that the pink panties don't go with the blouse, but I'm guessing you'd like to wear slacks or something else with the outfit?"

Rome was haunted with Romans and lions at midnight. The carriage driver slowly clicked around the cobbled street where the Colosseum's broken columns were lit up by moonlight.

The night was a hush of white velvet stars and summer darkness. The driver heard the steady low murmur of conversation and soft laughter behind him. He never turned to look. He'd been on this route forever and knew better than to turn around. He also guessed that his standard hour carriage ride might well turn into two, because they'd already passed the Colosseum twice and neither of his passengers had noticed it yet.

"We should go home," Leslie murmured.

"Yes."

"It's nearly one in the morning."

"Yes." Amused, Sam fingered her hair. Leslie was about as sleepy as a firecracker. Her face was glowing with triumph. She looked a picture of pure vibrant female and her lips still had the taste of just a little too much wine. She was used to shining in a crowd of men by using her sultry wiles. He'd watched her conquer a room of men with shyness, softness, and gently and carefully applied questions about their work and interests. He'd never cared if she conquered anyone, but it seemed to matter to her. In fact, it seemed a monumental surprise to her that she didn't have to play a role.

Her face tilted up to his. "And I saw you skimming that paper the man handed you, Sam. You were reading it just fine."

He nodded. "I memorized the speech because I already figured out that wasn't possible. I'll never be able to read aloud like everyone else—somehow out loud the words get mixed up—"

"Dyslexia," she affirmed.

"Yes." He didn't care what she called it. "But as far as the written page, lady, you know your business. It was almost worth walking the plank and jamming my nose to a blackboard for two solid months."

"Only almost? And we can work a little harder on that dyslexia, Sam. I can't even promise you it'll completely go away but I can—"

"Yes," he agreed. His lips got lost in the perfume of her hair. He hadn't been seriously following the conversation in an hour.

Neither had Leslie. Her shoes were somewhere in the bottom of the carriage. Her legs were tucked under her and her body had naturally gravitated to Sam's warmth. Any woman who learned to respect a predatory world early in life knew how to hold her liquor, or didn't drink. Three glasses of wine over a long evening had always been Leslie's limit.

Tonight she'd had four plus of the champagne that was now brimming up in a bubble world. She could never remember being this high. She'd coped with Sam's colleagues. He'd said he was proud of her. It had all been so deliriously easy and he looked so incredibly handsome in a dark-navy suit. She stretched out her legs, watched her bare toes tingle and felt perfectly wonderful. "I thought we were going to see the Colosseum."

"We are. It just seems to take a long ride to get there."

"I could dance forever, Sam."

"Could you?"

"I never want to leave this city. Ever."

"Then we won't," he promised her. At that moment he would have promised her anything.

"And we haven't even seen anything yet. I mean, Michelangelo's *Pietà* is right here—"

"And we've been busy conferencing. Not tomorrow. We'll go see everything you want tomorrow."

"Sam?"

"Hmm?"

"My right shoe just fell out of the carriage."

"We'll buy you a new pair of shoes tomorrow. Or ten. Would you like ten pairs of shoes?"

"Shoes are my vice," she confessed, "but that may be taking it a little far."

"You think so?"

"Don't you?"

"Not really." It was another thing she taught him that he'd never known before. How to talk nonsense. "So tomorrow we buy ten pairs of shoes and an ice-cream cone and see the *Pietà*."

"I was so proud of you when you accepted that award. All those people, Sam. They all knew what you'd accomplished."

"Are you going to get claustrophobia if we go down into the catacombs?"

"I haven't any idea and I want to talk about your work."

"Okay," he agreed. "This school you have in St. Paul, Les. Kids have the same problems everywhere, don't they? I mean, have you thought about starting schools like it in other places?''

She frowned and snuggled an arm around his waist. "We're talking about probabilistic risk assessment," she reminded him.

"We just did that."

"Did we?"

"And now we're going to talk about something else." The carriage was deep and dark and smelled of old soft leather. The steady clip-clop of the horse's hooves on cobblestones set up a lazy rhythm that blended with the moonlight and soft luster of her skin. Her eyes were sleepy when he tilted her chin up, and her lips were already parted.

If Leslie had ever been vulnerable, it was now. His mouth covered hers, wooing with all the passionate tenderness he was capable of. Her lips molded beneath his and her arms slid around his neck. The beat of her heart was so close. Her perfume surrounded him.

Her response was as innocent as the spirit of a child, all giving, sweet, total. Sam was...Sam. She didn't know when common sense had faded or what possibly could have happened to all her rational thinking. They were in cold storage for the night, that was all. Tonight she could conquer worlds with Sam. His lips promised her she could. The touch of his hands swept away all the dark corners, washed clean a thousand hesitations. How could she ever have believed she could live without seeing him again?

"I'm afraid we're never going to see the Colosseum tonight, love."

"No?" Her breath caught on a flare of fire when she felt his palm cupping her breast. She sank farther into the darkness of the carriage, into the warmth where Sam was.

"We're going back to the hotel to make love."

"Yes."

"Were you counting on getting a great deal of sleep tonight?"

"Not necessarily." His tongue found the hollow under her ear and she could feel the straining begin inside her. Her skin flushed. Her pulse vibrated the opening chords of a symphony.

"Tomorrow, we'll change our plane tickets."

"Fine."

"We'll stay a few more days."

"Yes."

"I love you."

"Sam, I love you!"

"And after that—"

"Yes. Yes."

"After that, sweet, we're getting married."

He ignored the razor jolt that tremored through her, and just kissed her. And touched, and loved, and caressed, and somehow got them both out of the carriage and paid the driver and maneuvered them both to his room.

She made love with total abandon. The first time he never did quite manage to get all her clothes off, but it wasn't strictly his fault. She was in an equally terrible hurry and he was definitely in no mood to argue. She turned to him like a woman obsessed with touch; she came to him like a woman greedy with need; she came to him like a woman hungry, desperate for love.

He loved her once, twice, three times. The palest sunrise was peeking in the windows when she turned to him the last time. Half asleep, all soft, her skin was supple under his hands, as moving and mobile as her lips. She whispered, "I love you," and whispered it again and again and then just his name.

When he woke up, it was past one in the afternoon and the bed beside him was empty. She was gone. He found her note ten minutes later.

Nine

"The ceiling on the west room on the second floor—"

"Painted."

"The copy machine fixed?"

The man with the shaggy brown beard nodded. "No sweat."

"Those old desks we picked up—?"

"Freshly varnished and in the rooms." Weaver propped a booted leg on Leslie's desk and folded his massive hands on his chest. "Leslie, do me a favor, would you? Don't think anymore. For the past five days, every time you think, I get a backache."

"Are you subtly trying to tell me that I've been pushing a little hard?" Leslie tried for a smile. Her second-in-command was a laid-back type who liked to believe he'd never graduated from the sixties. Never mind that he looked like a giant moose with an unkempt beard, Weaver was the best teacher she'd ever met in her life. For a long time she'd had the sneaky feeling that he could run the school himself, with both hands tied behind his back.

"You're so busy spinning your wheels that you're looking downright peaked," Weaver affirmed.

"Thanks."

"And while we're on the subject, I forbid you to take any more vacations. Every time you've come back from a vacation this summer, this whole place suddenly needs yet another complete overhaul." He motioned to the window. "It's sunny, the kids aren't going to be here for another two weeks, the school's in terrific shape. Everything that needs it has been fixed, screwed, painted, repaired, purchased or cleaned. So if you don't have the sense to drape yourself in a lawn chair for a few hours this afternoon—"

"I get the message." Leslie propped her chin in her hands and regarded him sadly. "Okay. Go home, Weaver."

He studied her for a few more moments. "If I thought it would help, I'd go pick up a bottle of grocery-store wine and personally supervise your getting drunk."

"Thanks, but no."

He heaved out of the chair and leaned over her desk long enough to tap his forefinger on her nose, not all that gently. "Smile," he said gruffly.

She smiled, at least until his footsteps faded in the hall and she heard the rattling echo of the front door closing. *Alone* promptly hit her like a bomb. The school was hollow and empty and lonely without kids in it. Upstairs, her private living quarters were even more hollow and lonely. She glanced at the enrollment lists and student files cluttering her desk, all representing work that was dying to be done.

For some remarkable reason, she had a decent chance to run the school in the black this year. Actually, Weaver had told her she would have run in the black the year before if she'd quit accepting students who didn't pay.

The promise of solvency was nice; absolutely of no interest to her, but nice. She rubbed the throbbing headache in her temples with two fingers and then stood up. Concentrating on paperwork wasn't possible; the trick was to come up with yet another physical project designed to wear her out. In the past five days, she hadn't found anything exhausting enough to keep her from thinking.

There had to be something.

A half hour later she was stirring paint, and a very short time after that she was perched on a stepladder and lavishing brush strokes on an inside storage closet on the second floor. School paper supplies were stacked helter-skelter in the hall just outside the door. Not that a closet necessarily needed an annual fresh paint job, but it was the only project she could find.

She was a third of the way finished when she heard the distant sound of the front door clattering open...then silence. Her shoulder muscles tensed and her brush strokes quickened. Several minutes passed before booted feet attacked the first-floor stairs. She sighed, and called out, "Look, Weaver, if you've got nothing better to do than yell at me again, you can just go right back home."

"He did."

Her head whipped around, then down.

Sam's eyes were still dark gray. She only saw them for an instant because by the next, he was crouching down. He had the lid to her open paint can in one hand and was reaching for a hammer to seal it shut with the other. He was dressed in gray pants and a white linen shirt, just the way a man who made his living at a desk should be. His clothes reminded her that Sam was a decent, intelligent, rational, reasonable man. Otherwise that quick glimpse of his eyes might have given her the impression that he was a primitive; unmanageable, dangerously furious. Her tongue promptly went numb. Every coherent thought left her head.

"You've got a spot of paint on your nose, sunshine," Sam added quietly. "And you're all through painting for the day."

"Sam..." Any minute now her tongue was going to unclog.

He stole the dripping paintbrush right out of her hand. "Where's the closest sink?"

"You can't be here," she said helplessly.

"Never mind. I'll find it."

There were two sinks in the kids' bathroom on the second floor, both of them a bright pink. By the time her legs had agreed to unfold from the stepladder and managed to travel to the bathroom, Sam was meticulously rinsing the white paint from her brush. She took the other sink to wash her hands. The sound of splashing water covered up an awful lot of silence.

"I don't know what you're doing here," she said finally.

"Of course you do. It's too damn tricky for two people to get married when they're not in the same place."

"We're not getting married!"

Sam laid the brush on a layer of paper towels and dried his hands. "I'm afraid we have to. I'm pregnant," he said blandly.

Any other time, she would have laughed—he clearly wanted her to laugh. Only not now. Her eyes mirrored both distress and despair. "You must have gotten the note I left you."

"Yes. The general message was fairly clear—that you wanted me to go out and find myself the right kind of woman, or some variation thereof. Obviously, I came here . . . as soon as I stopped being so mad I wanted to strangle you." He pushed open the door. "I haven't slept in the last twenty-four hours,

Les. You'd darn well better have some coffee. I take it you live on the third floor?''

He was moving too fast. She didn't have time to dry her hands. Rubbing her palms on her jeans, she rushed after him with some vague intention of blocking his entrance to her private living quarters.

She was too late. Her legs locked at the door at the top of the third-floor stairs. Sam no longer seemed in a hurry. In fact, his hands had slammed into his pockets and his eyes were dawdling over her one-room attic hideaway.

She'd never covered the slanted beams, just painted them. The walls were a pale cream and her couch the palest yellow. The couch was mounded with pastel pillows in the softest greens and corals and yellows. The same pastels were picked up in the Monet print on the wall and the standing screen that hid her narrow couch-bed in the corner. Sunlight streamed through the tall, narrow windows, dancing on her collection of glass unicorns on the lamp table.

Absolutely nothing in the room was expensive. Absolutely everything in the room was soft, feminine and distinctly nothing she wanted Sam to see.

"It's just like you." His eyes rested just a little longer on her narrow bed, then wandered back to her face. Her complexion had no more color than the cream walls. She was wearing white jeans and some kind of huge red top that seemed all sleeves; her feet were bare and she still had the small streak of paint on her nose. Her eyes were huge and dark and haunted with strain. No one had softer eyes than Les.

"You shouldn't have come," she said fiercely.

"I'm not leaving."

"You are leaving."

"Les, you can count on it. I'm not going anywhere," Sam said gently, and turned. Her kitchen was a pale-yellow alcove barely big enough to turn around in. A copper kettle was already on the stove; he flicked on the heat and started searching through her cupboards. He should have guessed she wouldn't have coffee. She stored four brands of herbal tea on the second shelf, and not one of them had caffeine.

He found her cups. None of them matched. All of them looked like delicate antiques, each hand-painted with flowers or leaves—not exactly something a man felt confident about handling when his hands were unsteady. Les was watching him from the other side of the room but she wasn't moving. He managed to put two cups on her minuscule counter and by that time the water was boiling.

He poured the water, returned the kettle to the stove and dropped down on the kitchen stool. He heard Les's impatient sigh. In time, she perched at the very edge of the stool on the opposite side. "You forgot to put in the tea bags," she said quietly.

"Who cares? Neither of us wants to drink tea."

"Go away, Sam."

He shook his head.

"I left for you. Not me," she continued.

He said patiently, "I'm about five seconds away from hauling you off that stool and making love to you until you can't see straight, sunshine. So if I were you, I'd start talking pretty fast."

A pale flush warmed her cheeks. She hesitated a long moment and then her gaze fell to a fascinating square of sunlight on the counter. Her finger traced the outline, and when she started talking, the words tumbled out one after the other. "I'm just not the woman you think I am. I never was. We're not just from different worlds; we might as well have grown up in a different universe from each other. I grew up in a house that wasn't much bigger than this room; my mother had no idea who my father was and didn't care. That's just for openers, Sam. You come from a world that has ethics and standards and morals. You assume people are good. From the very beginning, you assumed that I was good—a good woman, the kind of woman you would want in your life—"

He clamped his hand on her wandering finger. Fierce, dark eyes pinned hers. "How the *hell* could you think I'd judge you because of where you came from?"

"You should care." Her voice was suddenly shaky. She made a small move to release her captured hand; he wouldn't let it go. "In time you would have cared," she said lowly. "In time, you would have started wondering about where I'd been and what I'd done."

"If you're about to make up another fairy tale about the thousands of men in your life, Leslie—"

She shook her head. Tears were trying to spring into her eyes; the sunshine was just too bright. She didn't want to tell him; she'd never wanted to tell him this. She'd wanted to escape from his life while he still thought good of her, while he still carried the image in his head of a soft, vulnerable woman who wore powder-pink blouses and got lost in a sunrise.

"Oh, honey." Sam's voice vibrated with emotion. "Just do it, Les. Just tell me—"

"There were five." The words were choking her. "Five men, Sam, and not . . . love affairs, not something nice. I never even knew their names. I slept with men I didn't even know, one right after the other. We're talking one-night stands, and I did it deliberately. No caring about them; no love, no respect for myself or them. I was sixteen, and I—"

"God in heaven." The stool skittered back when he lurched to his feet.

She could feel his rage and see the pure black storm in his eyes, but nothing at that moment could have stopped the deluge of tears. She was scooped off the seat before she could draw in a breath. Her cheek was jammed to his chest and his arms ironed around her and she felt his mouth in her hair, a brand of a kiss. "Sam, you have to listen. There's no way to take it back, no way to make it right. There's no way I can make it into something pretty, something that doesn't matter—"

"Shh. Hush, Les." He cradled her up, wrapped her in his lap on the couch and soothed back her hair. She was fiercely rigid and kept making the foolish mistake of trying to bolt away from him. The great, choking sobs racking her were breaking his heart.

And she couldn't hush. She talked and kept on talking. She tried to tell him what it was like growing up in a small town where everyone was waiting for her to turn out like her mother. The stigma in school, the kids not allowed to play with her, the part-time job she'd had to beg for. She tried to explain about Johnny, who'd never really meant to hurt her. All he'd done was taken her to the junior prom and kissed her good-night. "Only that wasn't what he told the boys in the locker room, Sam. They all started talking and questioning him and showing off and suddenly his ego got involved and he had to compete, so he told them he'd scored with me."

She tried to make him understand what had happened after that. She'd fought so hard to live down the town's prejudice against her; she'd been fighting it since the day she was born. "But it was like they were waiting for me to make a mistake, Sam; they were just waiting and I . . ."

She'd lost her job in the bookstore and when she walked into the grocer's, the mothers of the girls she knew would look the other way. The boys wouldn't leave her alone; they'd make blatant passes in the middle of school, corner her after classes. And someone decided they'd better look into her home life and started talking foster homes. "My mother wasn't always there. Sometimes she'd take off for a few weeks at a time and . . ."

"Don't, Les," Sam whispered. "God, don't . . ."

Tears streamed from her eyes like a deluge. "I thought . . . I don't *know* what I thought. I wanted to get back at them. They were so damned determined to label me a slut no matter what I did, and I wanted to show all of them that I didn't care, that I was going to make it no matter what they did or thought about me. I thought it would prove something if I slept around. Only, Sam—it didn't prove anything and it was so awful and I felt so sick about myself afterward and I—"

Sam stopped listening. Listening wasn't doing any good and soothing her wasn't doing her any good and he didn't know what to do. He'd never known what to do with Les except love her. He pushed up her bulky top and dragged it over her head and flung it aside. She was trying to tell him about running away and lying that she was eighteen, finding a job and getting a general equivalency diploma and working her way through college . . .

"I *had* to be tough, Sam. Tough and hard—"

"You're real tough and hard, sunshine," he whispered. His hand fumbled for the snap of her jeans.

"Because of the kids. See, I know those kids even before they walk in. They're the kids nobody wants, the kids that have already had labels put on them—"

"Yes."

"But they're not really tough—"

"No?" He kissed her mouth and lowered her onto pastel cushions. He ripped one pillow out from behind her and then another two, and in that moment when he'd dared to let her mouth free she'd buried her fists in her eyes, trying to stop the flow of tears.

He kissed where he could, her forearm, her elbow, her wrists, the white, knotted knuckles of her slim hands. He kissed in her hair. He worked down her jeans with one hand, an awkward business since he had no intention of letting her get more than an inch away from him.

"Please don't—"

"All right," he agreed.

"You haven't been listening—"

"I've listened to every word," he promised her.

She felt the surprise of her own bareness before she fully understood what he intended. Her lungs were still trying to haul in air; her eyes were still blurred and her head was a thick mess of confusion and grief and old shame and trying to explain. From nowhere she felt the tip of his tongue on her breast, a rough scrape like wet velvet. Her pulse jolted in shock.

He didn't give her any time. His palm slid between her thighs and too fast, too intimately, claimed the core of her. Blood soared where he touched. She wasn't expecting...she'd never expected...

"Put your arms around me, Les. That's all you have to do."

"Sam..."

"You can argue with me for the next hundred years, honey. But not now."

She couldn't breathe. He wouldn't let her. She couldn't get control of her emotions. He didn't want her to have that control. She wrapped her arms around him because it was the only thing she could do, and he flooded her world with Sam—his taste, his touch, his scent, the sound of his harsh breathing.

Her lips sank under his when he drove inside her. Their fierce rhythm was like music, but not the song of guilt and shame that had haunted her for years. Not with Sam. That song just didn't work with Sam; it never had.

Her body arched responsively beneath him, young and supple and full of pride. His touch didn't erase what she'd done; it didn't have to. She loved him from her soul and there was the difference. The love was a rage of softness, of feeling start-over brand-new and clean with wonder. The rightness of giving herself to a man with love—he'd already taught her that—but this time there was so much more. This time she had nothing left to hide.

As fast as he claimed her, he turned intimacy into a tender taking. Her secrets belonged to him; he made sure she understood that. Her skin, lips, breasts, fingertips were precious. She surged beneath him on a tide of passion; he courted the rush-like pounding in her ears, whispered to her about loving and need. He scolded her with his lips for ever believing she was less than pure and good. Those kisses were the softest. He coaxed her to be wanton and free and abandoned for him. Those kisses were a brand.

She let out one fierce, exhausted cry in an ecstasy so potent it consumed her.

Afterward, she had a thousand things she wanted to say to him, but Sam kept kissing her and holding her and murmuring firmly to her about sleep. Since when had he turned into the bossy one? And she explained to him that she didn't need rest, never intended to ever need rest again as long as she lived....

"For some ridiculous reason, you don't have anything in your refrigerator but yogurt, sunshine. And you do have to eat."

Her eyes blinked open on a lazy dusk filtering in the windows and Sam leaning over her, stark naked with a container of yogurt in his hand. She propped herself up to a sitting position, disoriented when the pale-yellow blanket dropped from her chest.

"I figured you were starving."

"Yes. Sam, good Lord, you didn't have to let me sleep on like that—"

"You needed it. And if and when either one of us gets around to putting on clothes, we could both probably use a serious dinner, but it'll wait." He cocked a brow at her and shook his head. "You still have a paint smudge on your nose."

"Do I?"

He inhaled her smile, then nudged the white container and a spoon in her hand. "Want to talk children?"

"Children?"

"Are you awake?"

"I don't know," she admitted truthfully.

"Maybe that's just as well." He dropped down to the couch when she swung her legs over the side to make a place for him. The couch was long enough to seat four. They took up the space of one. "We have some fairly serious problems to discuss," he informed her. "Minnesota to Florida is the main one. You're very definitely committed to starting your school in just a few weeks. I can work out a temporary leave of absence, which will solve that first crisis—since postponing our marriage isn't an option. We're not going to be separated, Les." He waited, giving her all of three seconds to object before continuing.

"In the long run, I can uncommit from the work I'm doing now and peddle my education anywhere around most major universities I can think of. That sort of depends on you. I don't know whether you have ambitions to take your show on the road—start other schools the way you've started this one. I also don't know if you have anyone you could leave in charge here..."

"Sam." She waved a hand, trying to get his attention.

"The way I see it, there are kids everywhere who need you and what you've been doing here. Which basically leaves us homeless. I mean, very seriously, as far as I'm concerned we could start out anywhere you want to, but then we run into the problem of children. Our children. I want you to understand right off the bat that you don't have to be afraid of producing a prodigy. It's not genetic; my parents were perfectly normal people." He paused. "They're going to love you."

"Sam!"

He smiled for her.

She smiled back, and then set down her yogurt and spoon, none of which she'd tasted anyway. "I love you," she said vibrantly.

"This is no time to distract me into making love with you, Les," he scolded.

"I wasn't."

"Yes, you were. You do that breathing. Now come over here on my lap and eat your yogurt."

"I'm not hungry."

He sighed, dragged his arm around her and drew her closer. He didn't have to go far. She kissed his neck, the spot two inches below his ear that struck her as infinitely vulnerable. His chin suddenly nuzzled into her hair.

"I'm still angry with you," he informed her. "Very angry," he added softly. "You had no right to do that—make yourself pay for something that happened years ago. I care, sunshine. You were absolutely right in thinking that I'd care, but not because I'd ever judge you; I care about anything in your life that could have hurt you that badly."

She took a long breath and laid her cheek against him. "It isn't the kind of mistake you would have made, Sam."

"No? Frankly, I don't know what I'd have done if I'd been sixteen and in your shoes." He smoothed back her hair possessively. "You want me to tell you you were foolish?" he asked gently. "Maybe you were, love. Foolish and frightened and alone, and I wish I could have been there for you. Lord, if it would help, we could go back and burn down the whole damn town. I'm willing."

She shook her head, a glisten of tears in her eyes.

"You think I've never been foolish? That I've never made a mistake? Because if you've got a few years, I could fill you in on a fairly large list of things I've done that I'm not too proud of."

She shook her head again.

"And I never cared about your past, except as how it affected you, how it affected the two of us. You really think I can't understand about labels, about how you can feel crippled with the labels people place on you?"

She knew he did. Sam knew, if anyone knew. She touched his cheek and loved the shape of his chin and reveled in the love in his eyes. "How long is this lecture going to go on?" she asked absently.

"I don't know. How long is it going to take to get it through your head that I love you just as you are?"

"I love you, Sam."

"I know that, sunshine. I've known that for a long time, but that's not what we're discussing. We're talking about the light you bring to my life. We're talking about your taking on a staid and boring mathematician long-term."

"Staid? Boring? When?" She scolded, "You set me up from the very beginning, didn't you?"

"Me? You've been the boss in this relationship from the very start."

"That's what I thought—"

"And you just keep on thinking that," he murmured. Her lips were six inches away. Too far. He severed that distance and then let Les take over. Her lips claimed his, most possessively. She had a bossy tongue that knew exactly what it wanted. She reorganized every brain cell in his head before she was through, and he wasn't about to mention that she was breathing pretty heavily herself when he pulled back. "Anything else we need to discuss?"

"You think we could drag Harry away from fishing long enough to invite him to the wedding?"

"Yes."

"And kids, Sam. How about two? Or seven?"

"Yes. Anything else?"

"Not a thing." She circled her arms around his neck.

Silhouette Desire

Available May 1987

Still Waters

by

Leslie Davis Guccione

If Drew Branigan's six feet of Irish charm won yo[u] over in *Bittersweet Harvest*, Silhouette Desire #31[1] there's more where he came from—meet his hoo[d]lum-turned-cop younger brother, Ryan.

In *Still Waters*, Ryan Branigan gets a second chance t[o] win his childhood sweetheart, Sky, and this time it['s] for keeps.

Then look for *Something in Common*, coming i[n] September, 1987, and watch the oldest Branigan fin[d] the lady of his dreams.

After raising his five younger brothers, confirme[d] bachelor Kevin Branigan had finally found som[e] peace. He certainly didn't expect vibrant Eri[n] O'Connor to turn his world upside down!

For the millions who can't read
Give the Gift of Literacy

One out of five adults in North America
cannot read or write well enough
to fill out a job application
or understand the directions on a bottle of medicine.

**You can change all this by joining the fight
against illiteracy.**

For more information write to:
Contact, Box 81826, Lincoln, Neb. 68501
In the United States, call toll free: 800-228-3225

**The only degree you need
is a degree of caring**

LIT—A—1